ENGLISH CORRESPONDENCE

Sylvie is half French and half English. Since the death of her mother, she has written weekly letters to her father in London. When he too dies unexpectedly, she waits for the letter she knows he must have posted before his death. And as she waits, her carefully ordered and controlled life finally begins to unravel. Set in the Meuse—an area of France that is on the way to everywhere but nowhere in itself—*English Correspondence* involves a small cast of characters who move around each other in a complex game of emotional chess. Sylvie and her husband own a small hotel. He cooks, she runs it. Their lives are lived in public, as if they are permanently on stage—not ideal if your marriage is crumbling. The death of both her parents crystallizes Sylvie's sense that she has made all the wrong choices. But to change anything would bring the whole fragile card tower tumbling down.

ENGLISH CORRESPONDENCE

Janet Davey

CHIVERS PRESS
BATH

First published 2003
by
Chatto & Windus
This Large Print edition published by
Chivers Press
by arrangement with
Random House UK Limited
2003

ISBN 0 7540 1899 7

British Library Cataloguing in Publication Data available

Printed and bound in Great Britain by
BOOKCRAFT, Midsomer Norton, Somerset

To Charlotte Chesney

Part One

CHAPTER ONE

What Sylvie missed most when her father died were his letters. She hoped there might be one more. Post from England to France took about three days, sometimes longer, so there was always a gap between his dropping the envelope in the London post box and her picking it out from the pile of bills and flyers that landed on her desk. His death fell into this gap. She was certain of it. And when she was on the English side of the Channel, away from home, sorting out the funeral and other dispositions, she called her husband every afternoon and asked if the letter had arrived. This was all she asked. The telephone calls became briefer and the silence at either end recorded two quite different types of disappointment.

The hoping for something that didn't happen skewed the process of grief and her father remained adrift, lost in the mail. It was five years since her mother had died in the Clinique Saint Livier. She too had gone missing for a time, as Sylvie forgot her expressions and mannerisms, even the look of her face in repose. But after three days she had come back, not tentatively, completely, and Sylvie had recovered her way of walking, smiling, looking to the left when she didn't want to reply and a selection of coats, scarves, shoes and brooches which she had never expected to see again. This was normal. There were precedents. Lazarus four days, Jesus, three. She had asked other people and they said the same. The interval was similar. After that her mother stayed with her,

3

not all the time, that would have been intolerable, as trying as it had been when she came to stay, but retrievable in waking life and cropping up in dreams. Eve hadn't lived to see her grandson who was born six weeks after the day of her death. Her friends said she was willing herself to keep alive for that, but there are limits to will power. And, after she'd gone, they said, what a pity she hadn't managed to hang on.

*   *   *

Returning home in the inactive part of the day, Sylvie felt like a client. She walked through the low white gates that were always open and up the gravel path. The frames for the menus, to the side of the main door, were empty. She went in and put down the suitcase she'd been carrying. The lamp on the desk, in the hallway, was lit, guarding the essence of evening and dinnertime, marking time until they came round again. Outside it was bright and the illusion depressed her. She waited. No one was there to confirm her reservation or hand her a key. She knew she could stay here. It was more than a restaurant, though not quite a hotel. The food was what counted. She was resigned to standing there while her mind climbed the stairs and entered a bedroom, clean and silent, shaded by curtains. The pillows lay smooth and pale. Nobody's room.

From being almost asleep, Sylvie suddenly felt agitated. Why was there no one to help her? They didn't deserve business if they kept people waiting like this. She couldn't stand here all day. She needed to lie down; it was compelling. She knew

4

she wouldn't even be able to wait to pull back the cover. She looked impatiently at the high-backed chair and realised it was she who should have been sitting in it.

*   *   *

'I didn't know you were back. How long have you been here?'

Sylvie looked round. It was her husband addressing her.

'How long have you been here?'

She had been slow to reply.

'Not long. It seems quiet, doesn't it? Isn't anyone here?'

'No.'

'You mean they've gone out for the day? Or there just isn't anyone?'

'It's Monday, Sylvie.'

'I suppose it is. I'd forgotten. I don't really know what day it is. Where's Lucien? Isn't he here?'

'My mother took him home with her for the weekend. Natalie was managing but it's nice for him to have a change of scene. He likes the attention.'

Sylvie said nothing.

'Was your journey all right?'

'Not bad. There wasn't much traffic.'

'What time did you set off from London then?'

'About half past seven.'

'You stopped for lunch somewhere?'

'I stopped but I didn't need to eat. I had a cup of coffee.'

'I'll get you something, shall I? You shouldn't drive all that way without eating.'

5

'I've done it now. No, I don't want anything. Thanks.' She paused. 'What have you been doing?'

'Nothing out of the ordinary. It's been quiet. You were right. Even Saturday. It's looking a bit busier towards the end of the week. But you're not to do anything. Take it easy for another few days. I've asked Maude to hang on until Sunday.'

'Another few days. What did you mean by that?'

'What I said. What's funny about it?'

'You didn't say, for a few days, you said, for another few days.'

He was silent. Then he said, 'I'm sorry, Sylvie, I'm just not with you.'

'I wasn't doing nothing.'

'When?'

'While I was away. I wasn't doing nothing.'

'I know you weren't doing nothing. I didn't say you were, did I?'

'You said another few days. Don't you understand? Oh, let's leave it.'

She bent down and picked up the suitcase that she had put on the floor when she came in.

'I'll take that for you. Here, give it to me.'

She put it back down again and looked at him. He moved nearer to pick it up and she shook her head. 'We haven't actually said hullo to each other, have we?' she said.

He stepped forward and put his arms round her. She seemed to struggle slightly and then went still. She rested her forehead on his shoulder. They stayed there, then she shook herself free. 'I think I'd better go to bed.'

He looked at her face as if he were trying to find something. Then his eyes went blank and she could tell that he had remembered that it was pointless to look there.

She didn't go to bed. She stood at the window of the bedroom, in the part of the building they lived in. It was an implausible extension. From the outside, a leg to a body that didn't need a leg; from the inside, one of those surprises you find in dreams, an extra you are disturbed to come across and for which, when you wake with a start between five twenty and five twenty-five, you can't find a function. She tried to keep it separate from the restaurant and the guest rooms but she wasn't entirely successful. Things found their way across: white towels, the false damask counterpane on their bed, embossed plates from the dining room. She would have had to be a different sort of person to require strict demarcation, more assertive, more materialistic. She knew it would have been better to be like that, but she didn't care enough. Lucien's room was his own, a tidy child's room. He didn't spill out. He liked sorting his things and finding the best possible place for them. Natalie, the chambermaid, helped to look after him. She was young, more like an older sister. She had total recall of the register from her early school years. She recited it to him; alphabetic and nonsensical. Lucien asked her questions about the children as if they were his contemporaries. He wasn't interested in what had become of them since. Their lives had been uneventful; troubled only by minor illnesses and accidents. What Natalie couldn't remember she made up. She gave him unavoidable kisses and made his bed to hotel standards.

7

Sylvie unpacked her case. The black skirt and jacket neatly folded in tissue paper, the jeans, shirts, socks, tights, knickers and bras, crumpled, needing to be washed. Here, she had to be formal every day. It was part of the life, like the flowers on each table, chosen for their uprightness and staying power. She was at the hairdresser in the nearby town twice a week. She quite liked walking in there. The outside of the building blackened and ancient, the interior cool, white, noisy with music. The feeling of invigoration didn't go much past the threshold. Once she sat down in front of the mirror and Jean-Guy pulled his fingers speculatively through her hair, she simply felt mildly old.

She knew about bereavement. She had had it before. The feeling of not being quite well, like the after effects of flu. She stopped her unpacking. She had got to the assortment of things at the bottom, which all needed putting away but didn't have particular places to go. She couldn't cope with making so many small decisions. The quarter-read paperback, which she hadn't taken in, should it go on the shelf, or wait by the side of the bed for a second attempt? It was all like that.

Her mother had been ill for a long time before dying; her father had been old, not very old, but old enough for it to have made sense. And they were her parents. She wondered how it would be to lose someone you fiercely loved, whom you'd hungered after. She tried her heart for sharpness to test whether she knew what it might be like, but nothing happened. She had forgotten her son for a moment, then she remembered him, and felt sorry for forgetting him. But she had meant something different.

8

George de Mora had been English, whatever his name. What was left of the Portuguese had been in his eyes, sorrowful and sober in a way that the English didn't run to. So she had been Sylvie de Mora before the ceremony at the Mairie and other people's expectations took the last part away in marriage. She kept the 'de', however, as her husband made use of one. Delacour, all one word.

George had fallen in love in France, married, fathered one child and stayed for over forty years. He seemed, in every obvious way, settled. But when his wife, Sylvie's mother, died, he went back to England. He came to see his daughter and her family, three, maybe four times in the years he had left, but both he and Sylvie felt diminished by the visits and took time to recover. He slept in the main building along with the clients, stuck with the fire regulations and the Gideon Bible, daily new linen and bleach in the basin. At least the bed wasn't turned down every evening. They weren't grand enough for that—just a place in the country. Unless it was Monday he ate in the restaurant. He tried eating early with Lucien, in his daughter's apartment, but it seemed to cause too much trouble, so he stopped it. Natalie got harassed by the extra preparation and was self conscious about cooking for an adult. Paul's minor creations were served up to him in the dining room, decent wine poured by the waiter and placed out of reach. No giggling or talking. Sylvie hated looking across at him, alone at his table, and George wished himself back home with something chunkier and less delicious; bread on a board and a bottle from Oddbins. The difficulties of it all came between them and it was only after exchanging the second lot of letters after each return that they felt easy. The first lot were no good. Too much thanking.

Over nearly five years they wrote two hundred letters, something like that. One hundred apiece, shared between the weeks. They acknowledged each other's preoccupations but mostly they wrote about themselves and their own lives. Sylvie sent the first letter, writing to the rented London flat that George had found soon after her mother's death. He was determined to go. Sylvie was concerned for him and bemused that he'd gone back to England. Later he bought somewhere of his own and changed his address, but by then the correspondence had started. What was on the envelope didn't matter. When Lucien was old enough, he was included. His grandfather put in a separate sheet with slightly larger, less irregular handwriting than usual, but Lucien couldn't decipher a word of it. Sylvie was sorry not to be near enough to be of more use, but she felt the letters were a kind of lifeline; they kept him going. He also sent her books. She kept the current one in a drawer in her desk. They were like the letters, separate from the rest of her life. There were stretches of the day, when there was no one much about, that she could have filled with what Paul called administration. She was the administrator. It didn't have the same ring to it as chef; both boss and artist. She preferred to read.

Sylvie started off writing to George in French and he replied in English, nothing French about it. At home he and she had muddled up the

10

languages, changing about in mid conversation, dropping alternative words in. Conversing with her mother had seemed, by comparison, not exactly boring, because Eve was excitable and asked a lot of questions, but elementary and domestic. George persisted with the English in his letter writing and she fell into step, sensing that was what he wanted. He told her stories from his early life that he had never mentioned when they were all at home together. He claimed that he associated England with the humdrum, though his letters were never dull. He said his own parents had done their best to make wartime London monotonous; the hours when bombs weren't actually falling, at any rate. He felt safe going back there. Sylvie took this to mean that living there required less courage than continuing alone in France without Eve. Eve had presided over his everyday life. Perfect and exotic, she had been. He had never lost that sense of her. He wrote, in his letters, a kind of diary of his new life of coping, mixed up with bits of his English past that came back to him. He rarely referred to the years in between, although Sylvie had been part of them; not to his marriage, nor to his time working in Eve's father's business.

Sylvie had seen that her mother's illness cut him down. He wouldn't have said so or admitted restrictions. He loved her and willingly followed her into the narrower and narrower passage which pain and fear and the petty routines of hospital forced her into. He told her he loved her and talked of the nurses, their changes of shift, the way they washed and turned her, their skill with the drip and administering injections. Eve stopped asking about the weather outside and what he would have for his supper. Sylvie and George talked during her illness nothing but French. Even at the end when her mother couldn't utter, they used it to talk quietly over the bed.

*   *   *

In her time, Eve de Mora had been a great talker. She defined herself by the stories and anecdotes she gleaned and told. Although it would be more correct to put that the other way round. She gave you her news first and then paused momentarily and said, And what have you got to tell me, darling? Sylvie dreaded that pause. The stories came round and round, a cumulative oral history, the latest additions at the beginning. Sylvie knew she was part of it and wished there were a decent way of asking to be taken off the reel. Eve was a repeater. Nothing to do with old age or dementia, though it did seem to worsen. Sylvie wondered how to avoid it. Her own thoughts seemed to go in loops. They were unvoiced so they couldn't trouble other people, but the tendency was there. It worried her. Mondays, for instance, she always had the same thoughts on Mondays. On Sunday, Lucien usually stayed overnight with his grandparents and the staff were absent, so, for one day of the week, they weren't in a rush. Guests could stay overnight, but they weren't exactly welcome. Without dinner the place lost its point. She and Paul lay in a while and made love in the morning. The noises from outside got caught up with her thoughts. The milk tanker passing, school children's voices; the gate opposite clicked open, dragged across stones and clicked shut again. The inhabitants here led regular lives. Although she needed the rest, and kept drifting in and out of sleep, she missed Lucien and, in a way, the guests. The place felt empty.

*   *   *

Sylvie thought, today began differently, starting in England. There, she hadn't known which day it was. As soon as she got back to the restaurant, it had recaptured her, Monday, the first one of November, beginning at two o'clock.

CHAPTER TWO

'How did it go?' said Maude.

Sylvie had heard her car pull up outside a few moments ago and now she was here, in the hall, her clean morning face on, at odds with her scent, which Sylvie associated with the evening. She stood a few paces away, on the far side of the desk, looking and sounding as if she cared only for Sylvie, though the words themselves were casual.

'All right. You know what these things are like.'

'I've never had to do it,' Maude said. 'It's to come. My brother will probably do it, actually. He takes family stuff seriously. Always trying to get us all together. Organised games for the kids, races in the summer, treasure hunts, that sort of thing.'

Sylvie couldn't see how this would be good preparation for funerals.

Maude paused. 'Paul said you were close to your father.'

'Did he? When did he say that?'

'Some time last week. While you were away. He didn't come to see you much, did he? I don't think I ever met him.'

'No, probably not. He only came a few times. Not at all this year.'

'He wasn't fit enough to travel?'

'It wasn't that. He was fine, quite active really.'

'Messy journey though. Even with the Tunnel. It would have been easier for you if he'd stayed nearby. Less hassle.'

Sylvie looked at the clock, though this wasn't necessary, as it had just struck nine noisily. They

14

had to stop it at night and start it again in the morning. It was a nuisance, but added to the atmosphere. Time marked in an old-fashioned manner.

'You don't have to be here,' said Maude. 'I'll sort things for the next few days, however long you want. Paul said so. It's not very busy.'

'I haven't got anything else to do. I might just as well do some work.'

'You could treat yourself.'

'What sort of treat are you thinking of?'

'Something fun. Get yourself a makeover, or go on the sun bed. Cheer yourself up.'

'I don't think I'll bother. That kind of thing doesn't do much for me.'

'No? Well, we're all different. You're looking pale though. It would do you good.'

Sylvie shrugged her shoulders. She looked towards the window. The post van was drawing up outside blocking the view of the farm gate and the field beyond.

'There he is,' she said. 'What did you do with the post while I was away?'

'Dealt with it. It wasn't complicated.'

'So there's nothing outstanding?'

'No, I'd have told you, or asked Paul.'

'Did you put the personal stuff somewhere different?'

'There wasn't any. Are you expecting something?'

'Possibly.'

'Doesn't Paul mind? My husband would kill me. Only joking. I know that wasn't what you were talking about.' She paused. 'Well, if you're sure you don't need me I'll push off. Call me if you change

15

your mind. I'll come straight back.'

*   *   *

Sylvie listened to the sound of Maude's car revving up and going. She heard her brake casually at the main road and sweep to the right. The sound died away. She would drive through the village rather fast. There was nothing to stop for. Not even a baker's any more. At the far end where you might have expected the settlement to turn back into countryside and, where it used to, until two years ago, there was a house made of new bricks standing on raised ground. The earth still looked raw, the grass was having trouble getting going. It was hard to see why. The rain was the same and, all around, grass grew lushly, covering fields and sprouting up between cracks in the concrete. This was where Maude lived. She could have walked it, but she didn't want to. At least Sylvie always knew when she left and arrived.

The postman came in through the front entrance. A bit of the past that wouldn't carry on for much longer. Personal service, but not so personal that the man didn't look startled when Sylvie asked him if he would like a cup of coffee. He glanced back through the open door as if hoping for a sudden change in the weather, a pretext, maybe a blizzard. The sky was grey and high. The winters had been mild for the last three years, uneventful. He waited in the hall while she went to the bar to fetch it. He didn't follow her. She was conscious of his standing there, waiting. An outside person, who had got caught indoors. He wouldn't sit down; she hadn't suggested it. He

16

would be listening to the whistle and hiss of the machine through the wall. It seemed to take ages. She wished she was in a hotel at the end of a mountain valley, providing a refuge, making breakfast for everyone: the postman, the bus driver, the men with the snow plough. The last place of comfort and restoration. Here it was different. A restaurant with rooms perched on a slight hill in flat country in the department of the Meuse. The front of the building, the side where the entrance was, where the menus hung behind glass and the conifers were lined up in pots, faced the lane. Behind was a forest and beyond it, the plain, stretching for miles. That is how it was, but the position seemed arbitrary. Sylvie liked the idea of the valley; a mountain large and solid behind her, both safe and dangerous.

She came back into the hall, tried a smile and handed the man a small cup.

'I think I'm missing a letter,' she said.

'Where's it come from?'

He held the saucer at chest level and downed the drink in one. He opened his eyes wide and shuddered.

'Sorry, I forgot to ask if you wanted sugar. England.'

'That'll be it then. Foreign post. Anything could have happened to it. Probably at the other end.'

'It's never happened before,' Sylvie said.

'You've been lucky. Something special was it?'

'Yes, it was, actually.' She looked straight at him. 'I didn't take it.'

'I didn't say you did. I just want to find it.'

'What's the matter?' said Paul. He was wiping his feet on the doormat. He saw the postman with

17

an empty cup in his hand and his wife.

'Nothing,' she said. 'Nothing's the matter.'

'Thanks for the coffee.'

The man put the cup and saucer down on a shiny magazine, thought better of it and balanced them on a bowl of pot pourri. It looked pretty solid, but not really right. The cup slipped across the saucer and rolled into the petals. He hurried out of the door, slammed the gears on his van and was off.

'Why did you do that, Sylvie?'

She was silent. She knew he knew why. It made her sad. It never occurred to him she was picking the man up. That made her sad too.

'There wasn't a letter. We've already been through all this,' he said.

'I know. I couldn't help it. I wanted to make sure.'

'You mustn't involve other people like that. It's not fair on them. They don't know what it's all about.'

'Do you?'

He shook his head slowly. It wasn't a negative.

'And to be rational for a minute, Sylvie, even if your father *had* written to you it wouldn't have been conclusive.'

He began to flick through the pile of envelopes on the desk.

'What do you mean?' she said.

'I mean he wouldn't have said goodbye, would he? Just more of the same.'

He still had his back to her and seemed to have found what he wanted.

'Why have you been talking to Maude about me?' she said.

'I haven't. Why should I do that?'

18

'I don't know. You tell me.'

'What am I supposed to have said, for Christ's sake?'

'If you can't remember there's no point in telling you.'

'Oh, Sylvie, drop it. This isn't getting you anywhere. The bank has finally got round to replying to me. Let's hope they've remembered who I am this time.'

'What's wrong with wanting more of the same. Just one more. What else is there?'

He went back out again. Sylvie took herself into the dining room. She couldn't sit still. She scanned the tables for faultlessness, straightened a knife and patted a table-cloth. The staff had left it neat at the end of Sunday evening, ready for Tuesday. She was relieved not to be faced with the litter of breakfast. The clients often weren't themselves in the morning. They scattered crumbs and knocked things over. Their nights upstairs seemed not to have rested them. Yet they often commented on the silence, so different from where they had come from. Sylvie always made an effort to treat them gently, providing the sort of calm they might find in a hospital after the day staff had come on duty. She remembered it from the Clinique St Livier. The fears of the night were over, the beds made smooth and the pillows reflated. No sign yet of doctors, causers of chaos. She thought she knew how the clients felt. It was the time they most wanted home easiness. They missed slopping about in their night clothes, not smelling too lovely, listening to the news or reading the paper. The day ahead would involve too much driving. Most people were on their way somewhere else; this wasn't a tourist destination and no one came for the weather. The worst off were couples travelling with other couples. They felt honour bound to be cheerful. The women looked at each other's clothes with less forgiveness than in the evening. The best were the kids, noisy, not giving a damn, and covered in honey.

*   *   *

For the last week Sylvie had had breakfast in a café near George's flat. She had had to walk to get there, along the modest residential street and then out into a road, purposeful with buses and morning traffic. The fresh air had done her good after nights of inadequate sleep. She hadn't read, she couldn't concentrate, but she had liked being there, balanced on a stool and staring out at the street, or pressed into a space on the sofa between other people's open newspapers. She had taken a notebook and pen and written down what she had to do. There was a lot, but it had seemed more manageable turned into words. And her handwriting had looked almost dependable, on the French squared paper, slightly uneven, but not as bad as it might have been. It had been odd, indoors, in her father's flat. She recognised George's things, but not the place itself, or the way he'd organised it. She had only been there a few times, as it was hard to leave Lucien and the business. Paul had never gone with her; there was nowhere to sleep except on the sofa and he liked to be comfortable. She had made use of it again this time, avoiding George's bed. It was all right, provisional; it suited her mood. So there was none of the poignancy of the familiar. This is where he used to put his coat. None of that.

His chess-playing friend, Don, had been very helpful, guiding her through the procedures of death registry and funerals. She had met him once or twice on her visits to London and he had telephoned her when George died, to offer his support. He seemed to know everything so she had leant on him slightly and his authority upheld her without either of them noticing. She felt, although she didn't touch him, as if she were holding on to an arm made of wood, bent at the elbow for that purpose, joined at the shoulder but totally nerveless. He had arranged a meeting with Graham. Walking along to the vicarage with her, he gave an extensive lecture on the Church of England, explaining how, in its forms, it differed little from what she was used to. That at times like these the Pope and the past were irrelevant. He quoted from the Order for the Burial of the Dead in the Book of Common Prayer and advised her to be brisk with the undertaker, asking upfront about the wooziness and decrepitude of the pall bearers. That way she wouldn't be fobbed off. He advised against the outfit in the local high street and suggested somewhere in the suburbs where they were more punctilious. The wife of one of his old school chums hadn't been sufficiently incisive. His friend's dispatch had been rather dicey, made everyone nervous. Don failed, however, through lack of imagination and because he knew the man, to prepare her for Graham.

Sylvie's first mistake was to lie, which then confused her, and made Don thrust his hands deep in his trouser pockets and sway on his heels.

Graham asked her how long her father had lived in the parish and she construed the question as loaded and said it was a matter of weeks. She had thought, for a moment, that he was going to refuse a funeral to a non-attender. He nodded and wanted her to tell him about her father's churchmanship. This threw her. What had George made of God, would have been better. Wild and free, she could have said, or not there at all. Certainly nothing personal. He'd had enough of that in his childhood. What sort of churchman? Words rushed through her head. Lutheran, Huguenot, Calvinist, Jansenist. She was on the wrong tack. This was England. Labour, Conservative, certainly not that, something Democrat. Liberal, she said. So am I, he said, Good.

Then he came on to the readings. Had her father a scriptural passage, which meant a lot to him? He had said scriptural. She remembered one of George's letters. He had been re-reading the Gospels in English; the Authorised Version. He had quoted St John, the woman taken in adultery. Jesus had stooped down and written in the dust with his finger. Twice he had done it, Jesus that is. What I want to know, George wrote, was What did it say? She had thought about it. The answer might throw light on all sorts of difficult questions, or at least provide a further enigma to work on. But not to know. That was hard. Was it obscene, do you think, George had asked. It hadn't occurred to her.

She had the sense not to mention it. Even she, and in spite of the beauty of the passage, realised she mustn't mention it. He liked letters, she said. Ah, yes, said Graham. 1 Corinthians 13, that's always popular at weddings and, yes, at funerals.

That's the one with a list, isn't it, she said. How can love be a list? Even the unerotic sort. Graham and Don looked at her. She'd forgotten who they were. She had been thinking of George and the sort of thing she was able to say to him.

They let themselves out. Graham was juggling with a telephone and the proofs of his Appeal brochure. He sounded displeased. As Sylvie walked down the vicarage garden path with Don, she said how sorry she was. She explained that she had no experience of clergy, or, in a way, of the English. Her half claim through blood and her ease with the language were misleading. People assumed she understood more than she did. Don was disarmed. He smiled down at her, quite genuinely, and said they could probably both do with a drink, if she didn't think it was too early. There was somewhere tolerable on the tow path by the Thames. Graham didn't understand the ladies, never had done.

CHAPTER THREE

It was on the basis of that smile that Sylvie wrote to Don. She needed to write to him to thank him for his support and kindness at a difficult time, but it occurred to her thinking back over the last week, that they might keep in touch. She would find a way of suggesting it. She knew the lure of free dinners, or even reductions, to people on pensions. Not the truly old and frail; they weren't interested in eating. She would have to judge it. She wouldn't want him and his wife here on perpetual half board. Paul wouldn't put up with it and it would defeat her purpose. She wanted his letters.

She went to her desk and wrote to him. It was different from writing to George because she didn't really know him, but he had known George and involved himself in the funeral. For the first time, since coming back, she felt a bit human.

*   *   *

Paul's mother turned up with Lucien later that afternoon. Lunch-time at the restaurant had been quiet. A man and woman, on their way to Alsace, had broken their journey to eat. Just one couple always created hush in the dining room. Their conversation was intermittent and conducted at nearly a whisper. Once or twice one of them laughed and then cut it short. The sound in the unoccupied space was shocking. Afterwards Sylvie went to bed and lay down for an hour. She had wanted to collect Lucien from school herself. She

24

liked standing at the top of the sloping playground and watching the children come out, with their bags neat on their backs, or trailed on the ground, like uncooperative dogs. Something about the sight of the person collecting them reminded the children that they'd forgotten something and they ran back in again. Progress was always fitful; it was no good being in a hurry. Yvette had arranged with Paul that she would keep Lucien for an extra night to give Sylvie more time to herself. That's what they had said, though Sylvie didn't know what to do with the spare hours. There were enough without adding to them. It hadn't occurred to her to insist on what she wanted.

She set the alarm clock in case she dozed off. When it beeped, she got up and put her skirt and her shoes back on and listened out for her mother-in-law's car. As soon as she heard the tyres on the gravel she left the apartment and came out to the front entrance of the restaurant. The air was cold and Sylvie crossed her arms and rubbed her skin inside her sleeves to stop herself from shivering. Yvette, well wrapped up, inside a padded jacket, straightened herself up from undoing the hatchback and stood by, while Lucien jumped over the seats.

'He was one of the first out,' she called, 'and his gran was ready and waiting, having, I have to tell you, got herself the best parking spot at the head of the line, by getting there twenty minutes early. So we had none of that boring waiting around, did we, darling?'

Lucien glanced up at Yvette but didn't reply. They came up the path and Sylvie went towards them.

25

'He made you a beautiful hat out of red paper, Sylvie, very cheerful it was—to cheer you up. We got it out of a cutting-up book I found in the stationer's. Origami, that's a funny name, isn't it, poppet? We've already discussed that. I meant to bring it. I told him to leave it on the hall table, but he got in a rush and he *didn't*, but never mind. Never mind, that's what we said, didn't we? I'd have been late if I'd wasted time looking for it.'

'It wasn't for her,' Lucien said, though he kept an eye on Sylvie, as he spoke. They were all standing by the entrance and the moment for a proper greeting had passed.

'Yes it was, darling. We said so. I was all fingers and thumbs, but you did it so neatly from the instructions. I'm really annoyed with myself for leaving it behind.'

'It wasn't for you,' he said to his mother.

'I believe you,' Sylvie said. She kissed the top of his head and he ducked under her arm and ran into the hall.

'He's been such a love,' Yvette said. 'Any time. Really, darling. It's a treat for us and it gives you and Paul a bit of precious time together. You look cold. Let me feel your hands. You *are* cold. I'll just come in for a second and check a few dates with you. I brought my diary with me.'

Yvette saw Sylvie's face and said she'd changed her mind, she wouldn't bother her now, but she and Paul could have a little think about when suited them. Sylvie was to go in, in the warm, and no need to wave her off. She left rapidly. She always did, once she had made up her mind to go. Sylvie waved through the glass in the door and walked across to her desk. Lucien had vanished. For a few minutes it seemed to her that her mother-in-law was sitting on the arm of the armchair by the fire. She could hear Yvette talking, speculating, now that Lucien was out of the way, and they were safe indoors, about the funeral; that there couldn't have been many there—too many only children on both sides of the family to make a nice crowd. She would say, and not for the first time, that she simply couldn't understand why George had ever moved. His French friends, the ones he and Eve had made together, during their marriage, would have been such a comfort to him. They wouldn't have been able to manage the journey to London to pay their respects. Far too far to go for just an hour, and none of them young anymore. Everything was always so clear to her. Sylvie knew it was unreasonable to feel worn out by what Yvette was saying when she wasn't actually saying it. There wasn't much point in avoiding a conversation if she was going to have it in her head. But the unreal had an advantage; it tailed off once she'd got the gist of it.

She walked down the passage that led to their apartment, and listened out when she got to the corner. There was no sound but, at the far end, their door was wide open, making a bright path on the floor. It was wedged open with a large flat book. She waited silently for a moment, then she called out.

'Lucien.'

There was some scuffling from inside. He came running out.

'Go back and shut the door, darling. You can bring the book with you.'

He went back and tugged at the book, threw it

into the hallway of the apartment. The door slowly and automatically started to close.

'That's not what books are for, Lucien. It makes dents in them.'

'I don't want to read it,' he said. 'Stupid fire door.'

'I've got to go back to the restaurant,' she said, 'in case people turn up, but I haven't got work to do. No computer. No telephone, unless someone calls. You can keep me company.'

'All right.'

They walked back along the passage. The hall was still empty.

'Look at that.' Sylvie nodded towards her chair.

'What?'

'The cat. It's got in again.'

Lucien smiled.

'It's very clever,' Sylvie said. 'It's nearly the same colour as the cushion on the chair. It thinks we won't notice. Has it been here all the time I was away?'

'You were going to sit on it. Shall I sit on it? Gently?'

'No. You can put it out for me.'

Lucien gathered up the cat. It hung, large and inert, from his arms, face outwards. Sylvie opened the front door. Lucien hesitated and half flung the cat from him. It ruffled and unruffled itself and walked away down the path.

The telephone rang. It was Paul on the internal line. He was asking her if she had managed to rest. 'Yes, a bit,' she said. And when he asked her if she had got some sleep, she said she couldn't remember. It always seemed odd to speak to him like this, when he was a couple of rooms away. The

28

method worked for giving and taking messages, but nothing more personal. They had installed the system a few years ago but Sylvie still hadn't got used to it. She never knew what to say. She had memories of his coming into the hall from the kitchen and taking her by surprise. He asked if Lucien was there, and when she said he was, he asked if she could put him on—if she didn't have anything else she wanted to say to him.

She held out the telephone to Lucien. He listened and said, 'Yes,' then he put the receiver across to his other ear, then back again. 'All right,' he said, and put it down.

'I've got to go and make chocolate tart,' he said. 'I said I'd go as soon as I got back from school, but I forgot.'

'That's a treat,' she said. 'You don't often get asked.'

'He said it was to give you time by yourself.'

She nodded. 'I don't know that that's what I want.'

Lucien looked worried.

'Enjoy it. You will,' she said.

'Did you go to Grandad's funeral?'

'Yes,' she said.

He looked hard at her for a second and ran into the dining room. She could hear him call out to Paul as he got nearer the kitchen.

Sylvie walked round her desk. She brushed the cushion with her hand and sat down. She wondered if Lucien had asked Paul questions and what Paul had told him. He wouldn't have said much about George. Bereavement without a body was how he seemed to see it. Yvette wouldn't have mentioned him either. She liked everything to be nice.

Sylvie had got through the funeral. It had been less peaceful than she had expected. The organ was robust, as was some of the hymn singing, once the small congregation had warmed up. The church was locked for most of the week and had absorbed the late autumn damp. There were flutterings of parish activity: the notice board cluttered with lists for signing and pieces of thin coloured paper bearing information, the children's paintings pegged onto a line. Sunday, in either direction, was far off. Sylvie had chosen the flowers for their individual beauty and had seen that, from a distance, in the altar vases, they made little impact. She could remember the smell of the lilies and the sharp scent of the forced daffodils. Something about their colour had looked wrong against the altar carpet. She wished now she could do it again. Not just the flowers. She had been present but not present enough. Standing up, sitting down, kneeling. And although tradition and, in this case, the Church of England, did it for you and that had its advantages, there was a sense in which she hadn't been present and, in a way, not George either. Of course not George himself, as he was dead, but not anything of him.

She wondered, looking back, whether she shouldn't have faked it. The engagement, that is. By concentrating properly, being in the moment, even if she didn't exactly feel she was, she might have joined up the attempt with the experience, or, at least, narrowed the gap. She would have had to concentrate hard, and right from the beginning, from Graham saying, as he walked in, in a kindly sort of way and not too pompous, the sentences, I am the resurrection and the life, and one or two others, because it was over very, very quickly.

She had been surprised to see people she recognised from a long time ago. They bothered her more than the coffin. It seemed to her a coincidence that they should be there. She hadn't felt this kind of pervasive Englishness since she'd been a girl and gone visiting George's relations. It overwhelmed her. The clumsy way the women carried and delved into their handbags, the men's entanglements with their handkerchiefs, their non-committal eagerness to please, their worried smiles, reminded her of awkwardnesses she had forgotten. She wasn't like them. She remembered being twelve or thirteen; the feeling of being on the wrong side of a door. She even remembered the particular door, the English four-panelled sort, covered in white gloss paint, that looked so ship-shape to anyone not brought up to them. She'd gone to pick apples, or play with the dog in the garden, something that they thought she might like doing, while they sat and talked. Then, after getting cold out there, she'd come back in the house again. She had hung about outside the room where they were sitting, George and Eve and George's cousin and his wife. And her father was at home because he was English and related, and quite pleased to slot back into the rhubarb crumble for a short while, and Eve was the adored French wife who was never overwhelmed by anyone, least of all the comfortable English cousins with their huge biscuit tins and calendar of Devon hedges. At the funeral, the feeling came back complete, of being an equivocal age and size and nationality, of being a girl on her own, someone tacked on to her parent's relationship and not part of a family. And much as she wanted to be George's representative at his funeral, as well as his next of kin, she felt cut off, an outsider. Her age and size had been sorted out by time, she had stopped being thirteen and all arms and legs, but not the rest. She still felt alone. Everyone knew who she was, though. She had George's eyes.

Don and Judith had been good enough to lay on tea afterwards. The mourners were all glad of it, hot and sustaining, most welcome, though some of them realised that they'd developed a tremor since they last tried to balance a cup in a saucer. The spoons were abandoned, and the small bone china plates, with the cake and the cake crumbs at a tipsy slant, ended up in odd places, half way under the sofa and on top of the television. Once it turned five o'clock Don opened a bottle of wine. In many ways it was easier than tea. They talked fondly of George. They'd all liked him. There was no equivocation. They said he wouldn't have wanted to linger, or lose his faculties, or his marbles and they were partly talking of themselves, and one or two were on the way there. They said he had missed Eve and there weren't many marriages like that nowadays. That made them conscious of Sylvie. As she didn't have her husband with her, and failed to mention him, they were left uncertain of her marital position. She wasn't certain of it herself. Her father's death had shifted something. Paul had said he wouldn't come to the funeral. He would look after the restaurant and Lucien. She couldn't see what he was avoiding and didn't try to

32

persuade him. He made it sound positive, as if he were doing it for her benefit. So she made the journey on her own, lonely and cross at first, then she forgot him.

CHAPTER FOUR

Don's letter arrived a week after Sylvie's return. He must have sat down and replied to hers immediately. She didn't open it.

She held two distinct and contrary sets of thoughts about Don. She knew clearly what kind of man he was; unbending, inhibited, well intentioned, and most unlikely to write a good letter. Her father had chosen him for his ability to play a fair game of chess and his availability. He lived round the corner and had a comfortable sitting room. She knew, for a fact, that he would never tell her anything interesting. He would bore her with information, particular and general; holidays, politics recycled from his newspaper, planning permission and problems with transport. He would keep count of wet Julys, put a number to them. She would have trouble replying. She could see herself sitting there. Spontaneity would be out of the question. What could she ever want to say to him urgently? She would have to pretend to be like him to manage at all. And yet, after she'd written to him, she felt buoyed up, almost elated; though it wasn't real free-floating elation. She felt as if she had pushed herself against a tight thread that was barring her way, and that, for a moment, the pressure was so great that her feet left the ground. Paul noticed. He hoped she was coming out of it. The gloom she'd been in. For a few days they had been quite nice to each other.

The letter sat in the drawer of her desk until the evening. She thought of it from time to time, but couldn't face dealing with it. She used the words to herself, dealing with, not reading, that was too pleasurable. They had more bookings than they had had for weeks. She was relieved it was busier. The car park was half full. That was how she and Paul judged it. No one came here on foot. The village was separate, cut off by the main road and, in any case, dead. Clients were passing on the stairs. The ones coming down, tidy for dinner, vaguely scented, lightened by anticipation. The ones going up, lagging behind in contentment, the day's small desperations still hanging about them. Felix, the waiter, was late, so Sylvie was rushed, having to hurry between the front of house and the bar. After she'd come back from the funeral, he had surprised her by hugging her. She couldn't be impatient with him because of that and was simply relieved when he appeared at the door, hot and cold from his bike ride, breathing fast. He took his waiter's jacket from its hanger, put it on, looked efficient, shook off wherever he had come from, his girlfriend, the football, a fight with his brother. He took the tray of drinks from her hands and carried them over to the four men in suits who were looking up expectantly. There were still ten minutes to go before dinner. Sylvie suddenly felt she could cope with Don's letter; with having sent it, as well as what he might have said in reply. With her back to the room, she poured herself half a glass of wine from an uncorked bottle and drank it. Then she went to the desk in the hall and opened the letter.

*   *   *

35

Once all the clients were sitting down for dinner, the restlessness was over. They were tucked up at tables, all dining early, subdued, respectable. Mostly it was like this. There might be disruption at nine thirty or later. Dramatic couples walked in from over the Belgian border, careless, young, thin, blackened by fashion. They always chose minute or enormous amounts from the à la carte menu, without even glancing at Paul's choice for the evening. They wanted to know about particular ingredients. Then they ate without appreciation, shovelling food down, or leaving it. They drank cocktails and water, often just water, made all the others feel red faced and uncomfortable as they finished their bottles and started new ones. Sylvie always made a point of reassuring the frumpish diners. She smiled and filled their glasses, reintroduced the wine list. What she really wanted to do for these innocent, guilt-ridden victims was whisper, don't worry they're on something too, you just can't see it.

She was taking their orders, standing there in a proper frock, narrow necklace, tights, polished shoes with curved heels. She was cool but attentive, pointing things out, making suggestions. Some of them tried to engage her in conversation, telling her, God knows why, what they'd done during the day. Usually it was men that did this. Some were overwhelmed by their own garrulity; their mothers had admired them, let them run on. Occasionally male clients dealt in matrimonial trade-off. She knew the signs; the gaze never leaving her, moving between her eyes and her breasts. The wife overruled, not even able to say what she wanted to eat. Sylvie ignored the scrutiny and sped through

36

the order. The present encounter was different. She was standing by a table for two. The man had stopped speaking and was staring at her. His voice had been monotonous and he had tapped the menu in appropriate places. She lost all connection between what he had been saying and what she had to write down. She stared back at him. Her eyes couldn't leave him. They seemed to get stuck on his face; the wispy grey eyebrows, the half-moon spectacles that he was now looking over the top of, his pale tweed tie. She registered in a far away part of her brain that he wasn't attractive. It wasn't that. It was as if they were locked together in an unsatisfactory embrace on a dance floor, neither of them wanting to be there. She breathed oddly, too shallowly. She was unable to speak. She dropped her pen. It hit his wine glass, the large one. The glass rang like a bell and then smashed.

'How far have you got with your order, Sir, Madam? Perhaps move to this table. If it's not too much trouble.' Felix was next to her, speaking to the couple, one finger in the small of her back, as precise as a compass, pointing her in the direction of the door. She admired it and went there.

*   *   *

'Sylvie, what is it?'

She was sitting on the ecclesiastical bench in the hall, her head slightly bent, her hands clasping her knees. The fire in the wood-burning stove was throwing off too much heat. Paul stood looking down at her.

'I thought you were better. I'd no idea you'd do this. I haven't got time to look after you as well as

37

everything else. I told you to rest. But you seemed to be better. This last week I really thought you'd cracked it. Sylvie. Are you listening to me?'

She moved her head. It could have been a nod.

'I shouldn't have taken any notice of you. I should have gone ahead and done what I wanted to do. I blame myself, it was stupid.'

She straightened herself and pulled the hair that had fallen forward, away from her forehead. It wasn't a cosmetic gesture; she tugged it quite hard.

'I'm sorry. I don't know what happened to me. What did Felix say?'

'He just said you weren't well, you'd broken a glass.'

'It doesn't sound too terrible. Why are you making a fuss? I'll be all right now. You go back to the kitchen and do what you've got to do.'

'No, Sylvie I can't take the risk. Not twice in an evening. It upsets people.'

'How can breaking a glass upset people? It's always happening. They're not that sensitive. I'm going. I'm fine.'

She stood up, steadied herself on the back of the bench. She heard a car pulling up outside.

'You called her. What did you go and do that for?'

'Sylvie.'

'She's like some sort of mother to you. You can't wait for a second before you go crying after her. Is that what you meant when you said you should have done what you wanted to do? Got her here for the duration?'

'If you were more reliable I wouldn't have to. Do you think I actually enjoy asking her to come out at no notice in the middle of the evening?'

'What's she done with her kids then? Or are you more important?'

'Don't be stupid. Her husband's home tonight.'

'You know a lot, don't you? Does she write you a timetable?'

'Give it up, Sylvie.'

*   *   *

'Hi, you two. I didn't hear any of that.' Maude was already inside the door, one hand over the top button of her shirt, doing it up. 'Sorry you're stressed out, Syl. You got back to work too quickly. It's always a mistake.'

Sylvie thought, checking buttons is a reflex action at seeing me, or she got into her smart restaurant clothes too quickly.

'I'll catch up with you both later,' Maude said.

She and Paul exchanged looks, then she went into the dining room. Paul sat down and put his hand over Sylvie's. She was still clasping the bench.

'I'm sorry if I got cross,' he said.

'You got what you wanted anyway.'

'Don't say that sort of thing, Sylvie.'

She stood in the same position without looking at him.

'Are you still thinking about your father's letter?'

'I don't know really.' She sensed Maude moving about the dining room. She didn't want a witness.

'Why don't you write it?' Paul said.

'Sorry?'

'Why don't you write the letter he might have written.'

It took a moment for Sylvie to take in what he'd said. Then she felt as if she were in vast emptiness, caught across a towrope between two moving vehicles.

'I don't know where he is.' This wasn't what she meant to say. It was pathetic, too childlike.

Paul tightened his hand over hers.

'I don't know what he was thinking, what his thoughts were,' she said.

'How long did it take you to write to him usually?'

Sylvie thought, I can't cope with this. He doesn't know what he's saying. Maude must have suggested it, or his mother. He wouldn't have come up with this on his own. She could hear Maude chinking glasses together.

'Half an hour or so.' She pulled her hand away from underneath his. 'Do I write it as if he were writing it now, or then, on the day he would have written it?' Her voice was suddenly sharper.

'I don't know,' Paul said. 'You'll have to decide.'

God, thought Sylvie, he doesn't understand anything. She stared down at him.

'Don't dismiss the idea. It might help,' he said.

She took a deep breath. 'All right,' she said.

'Go and have a nice bath, or read a book or something,' he said. 'You haven't read at all since you got back. I won't be late coming to bed. No one new will arrive now.'

'I don't seem to be able to. Read, I mean. I'll go out. I need to walk.'

He watched her go to the cupboard and get out a coat. She put it on and left without turning round.

*   *   *

The lane from the restaurant to the main road was

40

too short. Sylvie knew from experience that she mustn't start thinking. If she started, she would never regain the concentration she needed to walk on the edge of the fast road, facing oncoming cars. George had taught her to do that, keep to the left when there wasn't a pavement. It was masculine, logical, but entirely terrifying approaching a bend. She would rather not see what was coming to hit her. At least at night she could see the beams from the headlights before the cars reached her and the time lag enabled her to press herself into the hedgerow, or straddle the ditch. She got to the junction. Two cars went past in different directions. For a second, one masked the other. There was silence and dark; nothing was coming. She crossed over. She walked without thinking. It was a trick she had learned from driving, shutting everything out. One lapse would slide into an accident. She felt the impact, before the thought; it kept her alert in one way, moribund in another. She liked the air on her face; that was something.

She reached the first house and the pavement. She slowed down and tried to make her heels quiet. She should have changed her shoes, but the back view of Maude in the dining room, and her husband sitting there, telling her to pretend to be George, forced her forward and out. That stuff about the bath and the book. So bloody patronising. As if he cared about what she was reading. Her coat was to hand which was lucky. It covered her up and made her anonymous, hiding her bare arms, her give-away frock. If she met anyone now in the village, she could just say good evening as if everything were normal. They wouldn't guess where she'd come from. A woman

41

out for a walk in the dark.

Dear Sylvie, Judith and I were only too glad to be of use. She remembered Don's letter verbatim. A flattening beginning. The might of the couple brought immediately to bear on her. The 'e' of Sylvie half enclosed, edging towards Sylvia, safer. Her own name sounding too pally, although it was French and complete. And Judith. What had she got to do with it? She had seen her at the funeral and the tea. Then the day afterwards Don had called round and conveyed a brief, and rather coldly worded invitation to supper. She had said no. She knew how it would be. The table for three nicely laid, Judith's cooking, Don droning on, bossy and prissy. The silences blocked up, airless, not spaces for thinking or smiling. She would say no again.

The houses here were quite close together, their fronts straight onto the pavement. They were old and patched up, closed up, though there must be people inside. The shutters were final. She had never walked by at the transitional moment, actually seen anyone lean out and shut them, or wind down the type with interior pulleys.

They were off to Judith's sister's villa for a break before Christmas. She lent it to them when her brood didn't require it. Only a small window. They seemed to have so many friends. He and Judith were well down the pecking order! They, the sister and brother-in-law, had taken the plunge when the children were growing too old for the 'usual family holiday'. It had proved a success. Congratulations, she thought. But it wasn't wholehearted. She was ashamed of the tone of the letter. Ashamed for herself. She knew what she'd done. She had

42

beckoned. It wasn't much, but she had done it, and he had dismissed her. He and Judith joined together in sympathy over the recent death of her father. This came after the holiday and sounded as if he'd never known George in person, just had the misfortune to run into the daughter. She should, he suggested, dwell on the, no doubt, plentiful happy times they had all had together as a family. Crash came the door on her fingers. She felt as if she had actually stood there and propositioned him face to face. Tous nos meilleurs voeux. Christ. Where had he got that from? The rest of the letter had been in English. Anything to avoid being even fleetingly, formally, Yours.

She stopped at the end of the village; it was a natural place to turn round. There, or Maude's house. After that, the pavement ran out. She walked back slowly. She still hadn't seen or heard anyone. The dogs were asleep and the sound from televisions didn't seep through the thick walls and shutters. She walked as far as the main road. The restaurant was visible, standing on raised ground, the forest behind it. The windows were bright. There were glints on the tops of the cars in the car park. It was some form of life. The name of the place was in blue lights on the roof. It had been there when they bought it. She'd thought it was hideous. Paul agreed but said the sign must stay as a landmark. From here she couldn't make out individual letters, just bars and rounds and diagonals. They used to joke about it. She said it reminded her of a fly electrocutor, the sort you saw at the butcher's.

*　　　*　　　*

43

It had been on New Year's Day, a year ago, that she first knew about Maude and her husband. Lunch was over. A culinary hangover cure, light and nourishing, and soon despatched. Sylvie had had the windows open all morning to air the place. The excess alcohol had seeped through the clients' skin. The smell stayed in a room, redolent of an earlier, cruder stage of vinification. Paul wasn't in the kitchen. Maude wasn't anywhere. Suddenly, for Sylvie, their absence had density. It was like a large unknown object, draped in a cloth, that she couldn't ignore. She had waited in the dining room long after the last clients had got up and left. At first she'd had things to do, so she had an excuse to hang around. Then it became clear to her that she was just waiting. She had given up at that point, as waiting was humiliating. When she got into the hall, Maude was on the bottom step of the staircase, her feet poised in descent. Her face was made up and her hair had had a good brushing. She smiled at Sylvie with confidence, as if she always crossed the hall in a way that landed her in that oblique, side-stepping position. There were two unoccupied rooms upstairs. Nine and seven. Both were spotless when Sylvie checked them. That would have been Maude. She paid attention. Even then Sylvie didn't know for certain. But she did.

* * *

The lights of the restaurant were still at a distance. Sylvie waited. She wasn't ready to stop thinking and there was the main road to deal with. She thought: in the beginning Paul and I matched each other in an understated way. Two overlapping circles. It took time to find out we had only touched at an edge that threw off a few sparks. She had kept hoping. She was sad that in the last ten months she had given George hardly any attention. She had written to him in a daze. She had collected things up—words, gestures, looks—Paul's and Maude's—put them by. Then they closed in on her. She glanced at her wrist. Dinner might be over. She had no way of telling. She had left her watch in the bathroom. She never wore one in the evening, just a pearl and gold bracelet. Her side of the swing doors didn't need precision, only efficient response.

CHAPTER FIVE

The next morning, Sylvie threw Don's letter away in the municipal bin. She couldn't afford distractions. Since George died, she had avoided tackling anything beyond the day-to-day running of the restaurant, but there were events in the diary that wouldn't wait. The most pressing of these was a big retirement party that she had known about since September. The client wanted five courses and bits in between. The 'five' was exact, as was the number of guests, but Christian, the man who rang her up, in the middle of the guests' breakfast, was hazy about things that couldn't be counted. Sylvie suggested he should come over to talk to her later in the day and make the final arrangements. Discussing food and drink over the telephone didn't work. People couldn't imagine themselves eating elaborate dinners out of context, unless they were properly greedy.

She needed the extra time to prepare herself. She had slept for an hour after getting back from her walk the night before. The cold air had done that much for her. But then it wore off. Her thoughts had re-formed like moisture on the inside of a window. She had woken and not slept again.

She found she had to exaggerate to get anything done. She'd lost the knack of carelessness, which is why, instead of chucking Don's letter in the waste paper basket at the side of her desk, she had walked down the lane to the huge blue container on the main road. It was the time of the week when it wasn't overflowing, its top at an angle and the

46

village cats balanced on the edge, tails up. She had raised the lid and dropped it in, then rubbed her hand on her coat. Don's platitudes had disappeared with the ends of bread and the cinders. She'd waited for a container truck, with a British number-plate, to pass, before crossing back to the lane. She told herself it had been a question of language. All kinds of things could go wrong if it wasn't your mother tongue; wrong emphases, misinterpretations, unintentional innuendo. She knew none of this applied to her. Her English was excellent. Because of George and the books, better than most. But it was a comfort to have an excuse even if she didn't believe it. It helped her to lay the matter to rest.

*   *   *

Sylvie sat with Christian, the firm's number two, and his secretary, to discuss the party. She was light headed from sleeplessness and might have been sitting an exam in a dream. But, having got rid of Don's letter, part of her felt cleaner, able to act rationally. They talked in the dining room round a table stripped of knives and forks, the white damask empty between them. It helped to focus attention and they could look round to conjure up the occasion and work out the details. Paul didn't offer fixed party menus for special occasions. He liked the clients to feel they had made the choices themselves. So it was up to Sylvie to make suggestions and steer them towards food that Paul enjoyed making. In the early days he had joined in, pleased and a bit nervous. But as his reputation grew, the occasions increased; corporate events

47

and birthdays ending in nought, as well as the traditional weddings, anniversaries and baptisms. The clients who were doing the choosing usually showed some form of neurotic behaviour, believing there was a perfect solution, but not quite trusting themselves to reach it. Others were just glad to waste time away from the office. Since Sylvie had come to learn Paul's preferences, the chef absented himself.

Sylvie watched Christian's eyes as they travelled the room. She could tell he could only see what was there. The simplest visual transformation was beyond him; evening for afternoon, presence for absence. They argued, he and the secretary, Verena, about what Maurice would want. There was a useful alliance between the modesty of the principal character—he wouldn't want anything too lavish, Christian said—and cash constraints. These had already been established at an earlier date. Christian justified himself with some serious nodding. The secretary was more astute, seemed to know Maurice would like a good send-off. Jacqueline, *his* secretary, had suggested as much. She was often invoked. There would have been less divination had she been there. Verena spoke for her. It was only once, after all, and Maurice had been fifty years in the firm. She was intrigued by the number, kept repeating it; her whole life could fit in it twice. Maurice would be lost without work, would try to drift back. She leant forward when she said this, looking compassionate. The more resounding the finale, the less likely he'd be to return for an encore. She sang in a choir and knew all about it. Sylvie asked about speeches. They caused problems for Paul, who worked to deadlines. The rule was to take the time people said and double or treble it. Sometimes she would have to send a message back to the kitchen: hold everything indefinitely. The speaker, it was always a man, would reproduce the years thus far so thoroughly, at such pedestrian pace, that everyone present feared their own would pass by attending to his. What a waste. This was often the moment when eyes met past the candles. Take it or leave it. It was life reasserting itself and often ended clumsily.

When they had left, Sylvie went back to her desk to write down what they'd decided. She was relieved they had gone. The afternoons were usually uninterrupted. She depended on that. The telephone might ring, or an early guest might demand keys, but they fitted into a pattern she understood. The hum of the computer and the clatter of the fax machine soothed her. She balanced her feet on the cross bar of her desk, kicked off her shoes, if no one was about. The pile of brochures showing regional excursions, the smooth stack of paper and envelopes, the pot of pens, the brass bell, the visiting cat, were all equal and equally benign. From the beginning she had felt more at home here than in the rooms where she and Paul slept and spent their non-working hours and minutes. Yes, there was the obligatory vase, but she stuck flowers in it that looked as if they might once have had roots. As she picked them from the garden herself, she knew they did.

*   *   *

They had bought the restaurant in the Meuse

twelve years ago with money lent by Paul's parents. They hadn't been married long then. Paul, having come out of chef school, was working in a hotel outside Toul. Sylvie had finished university and was helping out a family friend with the paperwork side of his wine business. She liked their tiny rented flat, its impermanence. The rooms were shadowy, overlooking a courtyard. The sounds of voices and the clatter of knives and forks were funnelled up the building and in through their windows. Paul was often back late, but she enjoyed the evenings waiting for him, co-existing with her neighbours. He was always pleased to see her and told her stories about the kitchen, in between their making love and sleeping. She was never lonely. It was the first time she'd lived away from home.

The previous owners of the restaurant had retired a decade after they should have done, relinquishing the business by degrees while still in possession of it. As life became difficult, they, the elderly brother and sister, dropped off bits they couldn't cope with. For instance, when chopping wood was beyond them (a technique they had perfected where she balanced the log against an iron bed head and he struck the blow) they found a felt pig, childhood relic, and stuck it in the grate. Or, when the fishmonger in the nearby town closed down, they simply dropped fish from the menu. One year, they put up a blue lighted sign on top of the restaurant. It was their last act of assurance. After that everything was a falling away. They cherished the sign for that reason, always looking forward to the autumn and the nights drawing in, so that they could switch it on earlier.

One or two of their own generation patronised

50

them, peering over their driving wheels, having trouble with the slope of the car park. They missed the fire and the fish, sitting there chewing tough meat in the cold. They were loyal but not stupid. Apart from these old ones, no one went there on purpose. No guide recommended them. Their likeliest clients were unsuspecting people who were already feeling hungry. They drove past and saw the sign from the main road. It was a testing experience, needing an interest in catching rum bits of the past before they disappeared for ever. No one stayed over. The creak and the curvature of the beds were congenital. You could sense it as soon as you walked through the door. Better to press on, or spend the night in the car.

Paul's parents had been delighted with the property. Bereft of the owners, it stood vacant, inviting enquiries. They had walked round exclaiming. Sylvie had felt uncomfortable. If they bought it, it would mark the end of what seemed provisional. She sided with the brother and sister and their makeshift arrangements. She liked the passage upstairs and its big flowered wallpaper, on the doors as well as the walls. There was a seamlessness to it that promised surprises. She didn't share this passion for improvement. She had thought, rather meanly, that her parents-in-law hadn't got that long to go themselves. They wouldn't see it like that. They would grow old, they knew that much, but not dippy; that was the misfortune of an earlier and less competent generation.

Paul's mother, Yvette, intuitive in some ways, had picked up her unease, but mistaken its source. She thought that Sylvie found the building creepy and would be jittery living there. She had telephoned often, while the re-furbishing was going on, wanting details of every last stroke of the paintbrush and, having got hold of the information, relayed it back to Sylvie with encouraging noises. Soon you won't recognise it. You'll forget what it looked like. Everything just as you want it, darling. Sylvie had felt Yvette was willing her to similar transformation. She hadn't been able to tell her that she thought the place was losing something, or that she herself would be losing her youth. She regretted having to give up their flat and the chance of trying out another one, with a different set of windows, and wondered how she would manage to work in the evenings as well as the days. It seemed enough to be married. She had fallen short, as far as Yvette was concerned, she knew that. Not confiding enough, then or later. She hadn't said what she wanted. She hadn't known.

While her mother was ill, Yvette had been kind to her. She came over to give a hand in the restaurant so that Sylvie was free for the hospital visiting. That was before Maude's time, before they'd built up the business. Yvette wanted Sylvie to talk and for her to talk back to her. She kept saying the wrong thing, but that was hardly her fault, as Sylvie gave her no clues. Sylvie knew that she didn't. Yvette imagined herself in the same situation; then, because she wasn't entirely egotistical, toned down the emotional content, made it emptier, in line with the way she saw Sylvie. It wasn't a good fit. She gave the impression that visiting the dying might feel a bit of a nuisance. An imposition that, if you were realistic, you could see an end to. No more problems with parking or trailing through hospital corridors, smelling that smell. The end was the point of the process. Yvette's own mother had died suddenly at the top of the stairs. She had got to the top and it happened. The family had assumed that, as Mother never usually went upstairs in the daytime, she must have been feeling under the weather and gone up for a lie down. The low-key logic seemed to keep them happy. It was quick and no trouble. The direction pleased them. Half way to heaven. Whenever Yvette talked in this way, Sylvie stared at her, shocked by her liveliness. Yvette was only a year or two younger than her mother and not dissimilar. Eve and Yvette. They looked different. Eve had been beautiful before her illness. But they were somehow the same. Maternal and ebullient. She had felt crushed by both of them.

Sylvie still had a sense of those late summer evenings when she drove back home from the hospital, heavy with the baby, but thinned out mentally. The road was straight and there were particular places where the landscape opened and she was aware of the sky and the position of the sun. The days were getting shorter, though not in gradation. A suddenly bright one appeared to reverse the direction. It was lucky. It was no good to see it as standard, let alone merited. Lives were like days. There was no point in congratulating yourself on your own health or longevity.

She would draw up in one car; Yvette, who was looking out for her, would pull away in another. Her husband Gilles would be waiting for her, wanting his supper. Sylvie felt she was part of a chain reaction of obligations, as pointless as an ugly piece of knitting. She longed to unravel it, or at least drop a few stitches. She realised too, as she changed back into her tidy clothes, that the exchange was deficient. Yvette was well suited to running the restaurant. She, herself, was a come down. All she had to offer at that time was an odd kind of sympathy, born of witnessing illness. The clients were all potential patients. She treated them with care, believing that she knew what was coming to them.

Her other fault was her failure to appreciate her husband's creativity. She couldn't see it like that, as his mother could. Or, she had to admit it, as Maude could. Maude had a way of going into the kitchen and admiring. She stood and asked lots of questions that had no answers, but flattered the respondent. How did Paul know that rice vinegar and unsmoked bacon were the ideal accompaniment for sea bass, or that the tiny blanched turnips would look so witty round the edge of the plate? She interpreted the clients to him. They were stupid and didn't know what they were eating. He was wasted on them. They were savouring every mouthful, speechless, clearly discerning. She was good at sniffing too. She had more than one kind. Quick, appreciative and launched from the larynx, or slow, with more of the bed than the stove about it.

CHAPTER SIX

They arrived all at once for Maurice's party. They came in from the car park and gathered in the hallway, struggling out of their damp, dark coats, that at the end of the evening would all look the same. A bright piece of silk, hanging out of a pocket, was good for cloakroom identification, otherwise they would be looking at labels and buttons and stray hairs on the collars. The smells of colognes and face creams blended together and fought with the confit of duck from the kitchen. Sylvie opened a bottle and sniffed the cork. That was better. Maude was burnished, almost refractive; hair, eyes, nails, lips, teeth, dress, stockings, shoes, everything shiny. Only her face was fashionably matt. She attracted attention. The men walking in, at that moment, Maurice's contemporaries, were, in age, her perfect admirers; admirers, not lovers, just the right gap. Loving would have tested them. The younger ones who followed were disturbed by her, glanced at her warily. Felix was used to her.

It took time to settle them down. They had worked out a seating plan in advance, but, even so, there were flutterings, minor disappointments, these more than excitements; perhaps they were past them. Some collapsed like blackbirds taking a sun bath, spread out and patient, some were poised ready to swoop. They all knew each other, to different degrees of intimacy. Nothing startling, though there was bound to be at least one pair with a secret, and others who had forgotten they had been close for a week or so. What really joined them, Sylvie thought, was miscalculation. They had gone into business with room for manoeuvre, clear escape routes. For a time, these were open, then they glazed over with shatter-proof glass. They lived in a fortress. She could see it in their faces.

Sylvie gave them a few minutes to stop fidgeting and then filled their glasses. It was one of those necessary pauses, like the one between Let us pray and praying. Get over the shuffling before starting. They turned to their neighbours to talk. To the right, to the left, best till last, nothing in it. One or two were left stranded with no one to speak to; they would drink up more quickly. Sylvie stood ready. Felix brought them their dishes. The first course. He did it neatly, without ostentation, avoiding their shoulders and badly timed gestures. Sylvie watched him, watched his hands and his speed. It was she who had taught him. Compared with him, they were babies. The menu planning had deprived them of choices. They ate what they were given. Don't wave your fork, Sweet. That's right, in it goes.

They weren't the only diners and, now there was a lull, Sylvie was able to attend to the others. There was an Englishman, on his own, and a couple, out to mark some exiguous event like a birthday. They had picked the wrong evening, but she didn't want to neglect them.

With the next course came Paul. He shook hands with Maurice and Maurice's wife. They exchanged congratulations with equal enthusiasm: confit of duck and fifty years' graft in the scales together. This was Maude's moment too. She came forward. She knew Maurice slightly and gave him a kiss, told him how young he looked. This was plainly a lie, but he smiled and swallowed it with his next gulp of claret. They had both been drinking quite fast, he and his wife. They were used to the quantity but not to the speed. His wife's fingers, pressed hard on the edge of the table, steadied the upper part of her body, but her head bobbed about. There was fear in her eyes, fear for the future, at home with Maurice. She was pleased that Maude kissed him. For a moment she hoped. Then knowledge of Maurice returned to her, she didn't need to look at him. She was a realistic woman. Had she looked, she'd have seen his high colour and the tic under his left eye.

Sylvie signalled to Felix to fetch in more water; the slightest movement, no speaking. He understood her. He walked round the table and poured it, cold and clear into their glasses. The candles were warm, melting slowly, one of them dripping. Maurice put his hand in his pocket, felt about. The pieces of paper were missing. There were his car keys. The first words, what were they? Despite tough market conditions, profit before interest—No. He shifted his bum, half stood up, carried on fishing. Sylvie looked on. She knew what was happening, she willed him to find them. She caught his eye, took a deep breath, looked serene. He stopped, patted his jacket. A slight rustle, like bank notes. He sat down, swigged his wine, forgot all about it, forgot all about her. What is it, Maurice, his wife whispered across the table. She was, as always, lagging behind. He took no notice; ignored her and turned to his neighbour.

Paul and Maude had gone back to the kitchen to beribbon the pudding. Sylvie went across to the two

57

extra tables. They were tolerant people, the couple and the solitary man. They got on with their dinners without complaining. The noise and the heat from the party were rising. These three were adult. They drew an invisible line round themselves. The couple found plenty to say to each other. It hadn't been an ideal choice for the birthday, but they didn't indulge in apologies or recriminations. Their measured response gave them mutual respect. Sylvie saw this and was glad for them. The Englishman was watchful. He had his own thoughts but the party impinged on them. He kept an eye out, looked slightly dismayed, though not necessarily for himself. Sylvie wasn't sure what he sensed but she thought she agreed with him.

Felix brought in the pudding. The sight subdued them. He had to dismantle it; it was that sort of pudding. He did it expertly. It collapsed and they fell on it. What remained of discernment and chic was undone.

Sylvie poured the champagne. The establishment had won in the matter of speeches. Nothing was to happen until after the food. Sylvie had been firm and Paul had been pleased with her. Maurice looked bovine. Panic had left him. The moment was near, but not now. He felt easy. The minutes stretched out.

Jacqueline, his secretary, looked round. Sylvie smiled at her and nodded. She supposed it was Jacqueline. Three shapes on the sideboard, two flat, the other a mound. Framed pictures for Maurice: one solemn, a local landscape, one jokey, some sort of cartoon of Maurice, neither accomplished. And flowers. She could smell them from here. It was the lilies that did it.

Christian, who had met Sylvie to make the arrangements, got to his feet. He kept the flat of his hands on the table, didn't stand straight, looked slightly aggressive. He started at the beginning, made it seem very distant, very local, very French. He, of course, hadn't been around at that time. The leaden anachronisms gave way to a list, then tailed off. Surely that hadn't taken fifty years. He mentioned bedrock and roots and foundations. He stopped just short of saying dead weight. The world was now global. He talked of relaxation and travel and well deserved leisure and being together—that meant Maurice's wife. He picked up his glass and proposed Maurice's retirement, long life and happiness. They all did. It didn't sound plausible. They were all fairly raucous, clinking their glasses. Jacqueline remembered Maurice's wife. She nudged Christian and whispered. They started again, the toasts and the clinking. Maurice would speak soon. They carried on talking. He'd speak soon. No one looked at him. A moving occasion. Maybe a handkerchief. They waited. Talk dwindled. No one looked. Only Felix.

Sylvie knew straightaway that the boy had never seen death before, or anything like it. She wanted to comfort him, hold him, send him home to his mother. But she was the wrong side of the table. She needed his help. She asked him quite calmly to get to the telephone. Call an ambulance. Tell them it's urgent. Tell Paul what's happened. Felix was pale but he trusted her, knew what to do.

The party round the table divided: those near Maurice who shifted away, those at either end who stayed put, exchanging glances and clichés, covertly

59

sipping champagne. It was the only booze on the table and the glasses were nearly full. Everyone who needed it wished it was red, or, at any rate, flat. They drank gingerly. Maurice's wife was confused, hoped her husband would recover without further bother. She clutched her hands together and kept blinking her eyes. He had been trouble before, but not quite like this; never in public. She came round the table to be with him. She didn't know whether to touch him. The occasion, more than the terror, confused her. Her wish, had she had one, was not that this hadn't happened, but that it had happened at home on an ordinary day. So many to choose from. Why did he have to?

Someone practical came forward, right into the middle; a woman with medical training, a course in the past, long or short. It was enough to give her confidence to deal with Maurice. Sylvie spoke to her briefly and let her attend to him. She turned and cleared the plates away quietly, brushed the crumbs from the tablecloth. The evening was too far on to be cleansed, but she tried. The minutes were long, which was dangerous for Maurice, but for everyone else a remission. Some of them talked in low voices; just phrases exchanged, not sustained conversation. The three on the distant tables were silent. Their appetite was gone. They abandoned their food and stared at their plates. They weren't voyeuristic. Sylvie respected their restraint. She wouldn't disturb it. Outside it was peaceful.

*　　　*　　　*

'It's here.' It was Maude who announced this,

60

hurrying in from the hall, on her high heels. They already knew. The siren, in the distance, then growing louder, the wheels and the motor, the tyres on the gravel, the jarring of doors sliding and slamming, ambulance doors, the same the world over. The paramedics came in with the draught, a man and a woman. They smelled of fresh air and canvas and rubber. Their colour was green; cold and practical, in the warmth of the room. Nothing else was green, only the stems and the scent of the lilies. They set to. Incredibly quick they were, wielding equipment, kitting him out. They left with the bulky form on the stretcher. Maude took Maurice's wife by the elbow, guided her. In spite of Maude, she was flustered and seemed to take a long time to get to the door.

Once the outside sounds died away, the party round the table changed shape. The space in the middle gaped, but at either end people shifted, pushed back their chairs or huddled together, flexed their shoulders, stretched their legs, started to talk.

'Have a fag.'

'I could use one.'

'Shit. This lighter's buggered.'

'Use the candle.'

'Cheers.'

'Christ. What an evening.'

'Poor sod.'

'Poor old Maurice.'

'He didn't deserve this.'

'Not this way.'

Sylvie hung back from the table. They didn't want her. They needed to pretend that the restaurant had vanished and they were back in the office.

'Didn't look too clever, did he?'

'What are his chances?'

'Not great. Can't be, can they?'

'Gone already, I thought.'

'You can tell from the colour.'

'It was too much for him.'

'The strain of the evening.'

'The thought of retiring.'

'He didn't want to.'

'Looks like he won't have to.'

'How old *was* he?'

'Must have been seventy.'

'Over, surely.'

'He got overwrought.'

'Very emotional.'

'Heavy on the drink.'

'I noticed that.'

'Bad business.'

'Bad for his wife.'

'I can't believe it, I just can't believe it.'

'He just keeled over.'

'Pissed himself.'

'Did he?'

'Here comes the coffee.'

Paul had come in looking oddly patrician, Maude in his wake with a tray. He spoke to a few of them, as he went round the table: well-chosen words, fairly grave. He didn't say drinks on the house, but this was implied. He took orders for spirits. They were all takers.

They relaxed, talked about different things, started to laugh. There was no music, but they all heard it playing, rhythmic and steady, faintly suggestive.

It was half past one when they left. Maude and the boy who helped in the kitchen had already gone home. Sylvie found coats and helped people into them. One or two bungled it. A heavy man tried to get into a thin woman's coat. Too short in the arm; that's how he knew. Sylvie held her breath as they reversed in the car park, but it turned out all right. Paul usually idled around the kitchen, checking the knives and listening to the radio; music from earlier decades, nothing anyone remembered, B movie stuff, interrupted by histrionic news. Tonight when Sylvie went to find him, the place was dark. Sylvie and Felix opened the windows in the dining room, got out the mop and the bucket. It didn't take them long. Felix had thrown up in the toilet a few hours before, then felt better. He was young. She saw him off on his bike, watched him freewheeling down the hill. She locked up, shut the windows, turned the lights off.

CHAPTER SEVEN

The Englishman, who had dined alone, came down for breakfast at eight o'clock. He sat down at a corner table, the only client in the room. The scene was different—tidy, silent, slightly chilly, lit by daylight. Sylvie, glancing in the mirror, saw that she looked tired. She said she hoped he hadn't been disturbed by the noise of the party leaving; it had all gone on much later than she had expected. He said he'd slept through it. He sounded definite about it. She saw him there sleeping. He had conjured himself up. It disturbed her. She remembered that she had thought about him before falling asleep herself. He couldn't possibly know that. She was sure he couldn't. Yet he was capable of thinking, she could tell, in a way that most people weren't. She'd seen that last night. He'd sat through the drama with restraint. He wouldn't dine out on it, make it into an anecdote. George could put on a voice for a certain type of Englishman. God, what an evening, in the middle of nowhere, back of beyond, bunch of provincials. One of them pegged it. Ruined my dinner.

He had got up from his table soon after they had taken Maurice away. The birthday couple had stayed on a little longer. Sylvie had gone across to him to say she was sorry, though this wasn't quite appropriate, and to wish him good night, which didn't seem right either. He had accepted both decently, aware of her difficulties, somehow conveying that. She had been grateful. She hadn't expected such consideration. She had watched him

64

climb the first few stairs then turned away.

When she got to her own room at the end of the evening the light was off. She undressed in the dark, lay down on the bed. The slight disturbance must have woken Paul. She could see his eyes; they weren't shut. He asked her what she was doing on top of the covers, it was winter wasn't it? He gathered her under, said she felt cold, which she was. He felt hard against her. She registered pleasure and anticipation, but couldn't stop herself thinking that this was unusual, a throwback. They didn't make love at night any more. The kitchen wilted him. It hadn't in the past, but she couldn't put a date on it. She thought, the disaster's revived him; death on the premises. George's hadn't done anything for him. The thinking took seconds, and was over dramatic. The moment passed. Timing was everything these days. He rolled over away from her, fell asleep instantly. She lay on her side, her face pressed on her arm. She was so tired she hardly noticed her flesh was her own. It was then that she thought of him; the solitary man at the table. Her thoughts weren't particular.

*   *   *

She poured him more coffee; it was the least she could do. He had only booked in for one night, so he would be gone in three hours. They asked clients to leave by eleven. It was written on the form on the backs of the doors. She had filled in the numbers herself, the times for breakfast and leaving, in her French school handwriting, so different from George's. She didn't say any more, or ask him questions about himself, or where he was going. It seemed impertinent. And, in a sense, she didn't want to know. That wasn't the sort of conversation she wanted. She had trouble with questions. Such a high level of intrusion for a banal response. She didn't like them, so it didn't seem right to inflict them on other people.

The couple came down and sat by the window, commented on the rain on the hedge and the state of the sky. They were hungry. Sylvie wasn't surprised. They hadn't finished their dinners. She sliced up more bread and brought it across to them. She stopped and chatted to them. They were easy to talk to and she suddenly wanted to. When she moved away she saw that the Englishman had left the room. She hadn't noticed him going. She looked across at his table, the plate with a smear of butter on the edge, the empty cup. It could wait. She didn't feel able to clear it away.

*   *   *

Paul was by her desk when the man came to check out. He'd driven Lucien to school. There and back took about half an hour. He moved his hand slightly, indicating that Sylvie could sort out the bill. She got on with doing it but ignored the gesture. It was strange that this was possible. It required concentration and made her feel feverish.

'Come and stay here again when there's less going on.' Paul took up a position that almost obscured her. 'It's normally pleasantly dull here. Relaxing.' He smiled. 'We like our guests to concentrate on the food. That's what we're here for.' He glanced across at the dining room door, wide open and letting light into the hall. 'They

66

were unusually difficult circumstances. I hope my wife looked after you.'

The man nodded, not looking at either of them.

'We don't know the outcome,' said Paul. 'Whether the resuscitation succeeded.'

Sylvie kept her head down. He never even asked, she thought, he wouldn't, why should he? She remembered that George had once written to her and said that if he were ever taken to hospital he wanted DNR tied to the bed. They only understand acronyms, he wrote, so don't bother to spell it out, though, in case you don't know, it means, do not resuscitate. Don't dwell on it though, I just wanted to mention it. It hadn't been necessary.

'Have you got far to drive?' Paul asked

'Calais, then London.'

'It's not a bad day. Drying up. The couple who were also staying last night, the others who got caught up in this, they're leaving too. They haven't got far to go, over towards Metz.'

The man nodded. Sylvie handed him his bill. He read it and paid it, looked briefly at her.

'Have a good journey,' Paul said. 'I hope we'll see you again. We'll make sure it's more cheerful next time.'

'I'll go and clear up,' Sylvie said.

She came round from her side of the desk, walked across the room and through into the dining room without turning her head. She felt the cold damp air come in, as the Englishman opened the front door and went out. The telephone rang. She was glad. She didn't want to hear the sound of his car starting up, going away. She had, for half a second, wondered how she was going to shut it out.

' 'Phone, Sylvie,' Paul called from the hall.

67

'Can't you answer it?'

She could hear him muttering. But he was standing right next to it. Why couldn't he answer it?

'It will be for you, Sylvie.'

'Let it ring then.' For as long as it takes for the car to go, she thought.

'You're bloody rude.' But he picked it up. She hoped. All she could hear was Paul's voice. No sounds from outside. That was all right.

*   *   *

She was methodical in her tidying. She followed a routine that left her otherwise free. The last thing to be done was to shake out the clean linen, square it up on the tables, smooth it flat. She usually liked this moment, creating expanses of smoothness, but today she didn't stop for it. She walked away quickly. Before she got to the door she turned and looked down the length of the room. She saw it as it was, empty and everyday, but in the middle of the long table was the place where Maurice had slumped in his chair. He had gone to a position of weakness that was death and people had straightaway taken advantage of it. First his colleagues, then Paul. It seemed to restore them to talk about it and because they weren't close to him they felt no pain. It was like taking a drug with no side effects. There must be side effects, Sylvie thought, though she couldn't at the moment work out why no one was suffering from them. She closed her eyes. When she opened them she was careful not to look back in that direction. She stared instead at the corner where the Englishman had been sitting. There was a book on the floor.

*   *   *

Paul had gone. He had left a message on the desk with many underlinings. Everything was underlined, she now saw. This was to show that she should have taken the call. It was a booking: her affair. She sat down, switched the computer on, waited, typed in the entry, a week on Friday, dinner for four and two double rooms. She looked at the screen, but felt the book on her lap.

She had never read it, though the title was familiar. George might have mentioned it. She couldn't ask him about it now, whether he thought it worth reading. She would read it anyway. She wanted to. She picked it up, glanced inside the front cover. It was blank. There was some sort of bookmark. She opened it cautiously, not wanting to lose his place. It was an envelope, a blue one. She turned it over. There were lines of writing, not entirely even, slanting downwards, the ink was blue-black, old-fashioned, real ink. The writer was old, probably female. The stamp was first class and the postmark was smudged. She examined it carefully, trying to disregard the fact that there in front of her were the Englishman's name and address.

She put the envelope to one side by her right elbow and opened the book at the page that he'd got to.

A bachelor's loneliness is a private affair of his own; he hasn't to look into a face to be ashamed of feeling it and inflicting it at the

69

same time; 'tis his pillow; he can punch it an he pleases, and turn it over t' other side, if he's for a mighty variation; there's a dream in it. But our poor couple are staring wide awake. All their dreaming's done. They've emptied their bottle of elixir, or broken it; and she has a thirst for the use of the tongue, and he to yawn with a crony; and they may converse, they're not aware of it, more than the desert that has drunk a shower. So as soon as possible she's away to the ladies, and he puts on his Club. That's what your bachelor sees and would like to spare them; and if he didn't see something of the sort he'd be off with a noose round his neck, on his knees in the dew to the morning milkmaid.

'Did you see my message? I left it on the desk for you.'

Sylvie jumped.

'You were miles away, weren't you? Did you see it?' Paul said.

'Yes. That was fine. Thank you.'

'It's good to see you reading again. You must be feeling more yourself.'

'Maybe.' *Feeling it and inflicting it*, Sylvie thought. What she read haphazardly made more sense than what he said to her. In a different century she would have been one of those women who stuck a pin in the Bible to find out what to do next.

'Is it one of your father's old books? Or have you reverted to French?'

She considered for a moment. 'No. I found it in the dining room. The Englishman, who was here, left it behind. He must have been reading it.'

'You were deep in it. It's obviously your sort of thing.'

Sylvie shrugged. 'I don't know really. I've only just opened it. In the middle.'

'I thought I'd call the hospital and find out about Maurice. It would be a good thing to do, wouldn't it?' he said.

'If you want to. I wouldn't.'

'Why not? Why wouldn't you?'

'Seems a bit funny. Nosy. We'll hear soon enough. Why do we need to know?'

'It's courteous, isn't it, to show an interest? If he's definitely died we can send flowers.'

'His wife left her flowers behind yesterday. I put them in a bucket of water and left them by the back door.'

'What's that got to do with anything?'

'Nothing. I just thought I'd mention it. You said flowers and I thought of it.'

'You didn't think we could send them, did you? If he's died.'

'No, of course not.'

'I never know with you.'

'Thanks.'

'I'm sorry I interrupted you. I won't call the hospital if it's such a crass thing to do. You make yourself quite clear you know.'

Sylvie didn't say anything. She couldn't understand this fascination with the boundary, whether Maurice had crossed or re-crossed it. Was this what Paul and the others hoped for themselves? A permeable layer at the end of their lives where they could be dragged to and fro. Maurice couldn't have looked as he did and come back.

71

'I'll let you get on with your English studies. They demolished the cheese yesterday. You'll have to put in an early order.'

'I might send it to him. That might be best.'

'What?'

'The book.'

'To Maurice?'

'No, of course not. To the man who left it behind.'

'You don't know where to send it.'

'I can find out.'

'What was his name?'

'George Meredith. No, sorry. That's the name of the writer. I'll find out. It will be on file.'

'I wouldn't go to the trouble. He won't miss it.'

'I'll see. People like their books back.'

'Please yourself. What's it about anyway, that you were so fascinated by it?'

She wondered for a moment whether to read aloud selectively to him. *And she has a thirst for the use of the tongue.* The translation would be difficult to get right. *On his knees in the dew to the morning milkmaid.* That would be more straightforward once she remembered the word for milkmaid in French. Something stopped her. From time to time, Paul read books that contained precise physiological sex, but he resisted suggestion, particularly, it seemed, if she was doing the suggesting. Not that she'd tried for a while. She looked at the passages in these books without being moved; they were like attempts to describe a piece of music by writing about the movements of the leader's bowing arm.

'The bit I was reading was about a bachelor. I don't know about the rest.'

72

'That figures.'

'Sorry?'

'It's what he would read about. A lone Englishman. He's probably a pederast.'

'Probably.'

CHAPTER EIGHT

Sylvie wasn't a strategist. Although reserved she acted on impulse. So that afternoon, when her mother-in-law spoke to her on the telephone and said she had an hour or two free and was about to come over, Sylvie said that Paul was out, she didn't know where he was, and that she would rather Yvette didn't, as she needed some time to herself. But, darling, Yvette said, it's you I want to see too, you know, I like seeing you on your own. Brooding is so destructive. You need to get out of yourself. What do you need this time alone *for*? What good does it do? You need company.

She came over.

*   *   *

She and Gilles lived about forty-five minutes' drive away; near enough for them never under any circumstances to have to stay. The second half of Yvette's second glass of wine always remained complacently on the table. They were proprietorial about the restaurant, having put up the money, though not excessively so, as they realised this was bad manners. Apart from casual visits they came for special dinners at Paul's invitation; anniversaries, birthdays, mothers' days, name days. The year was full of them and, by a fluke, they were evenly spaced, so that it wasn't possible for Sylvie to recoup in an off season. Yvette saw it differently. There was always something to look forward to. At the end of these occasions they swept off in their

74

car. Not for them the anonymity of the hotel bedroom that George had had to put up with.

Sylvie suggested that the two of them went for a walk. Natalie could be in charge for an hour. She knew from experience that this would be easier than sitting cosy at home. If the conversation got tricky she could always draw attention to the surroundings; the scene in motion, the smell of the pines. It was less blatant than changing the subject. Yvette picked up on that.

'Which way shall we go then, darling?'

'You choose,' Sylvie said. 'Forest? If your shoes are all right. It could be muddy.'

She wasn't up to shepherding Yvette along the main road. They set off. The track was wide, made of compacted earth and decades of needles, the trees either side densely packed. There was order here, though Sylvie had no key to it. Every felled tree had a number attached to it. When she looked up there was plenty of sky.

'My feet are fine,' said Yvette. 'Where does it go to?'

'Go to?'

'The path.'

'I don't know really. I've brought you here before, haven't I? It seems to go on. The tracks don't have signposts. It's not done up for hikers. The foresters know their way around. I suppose if you keep going you come out at a road or a village. But I've never done it. The mist has cleared now. We should be able to see where we're going.'

'I thought there might be a view, or a place to sit down. It's nice to have something to aim for and then you know when to turn round.'

Sylvie thought, why does that sort of comment

75

annoy me so much? It was the certainty not the triteness that bothered her. She wanted to say, I much prefer going round in wide circles, and, on a good day, I might even get lost. It didn't need effort. Getting lost just happened. It all looked the same.

'If we had gone on the other walk there would have been an end point,' she said.

'What's that, darling?'

'Maude's house.'

Yvette blinked and smiled, switched off the smile as soon as it had begun. Sylvie knew she shouldn't have said it, but sometimes she liked to disconcert her. Perhaps they should have gone that way. Paul's car parked outside. It probably wasn't, but it might have been. With Yvette there. Almost worth doing.

*   *   *

'Are you going back to London?' Yvette said.

Sylvie realised that the other subject was now out of bounds. It might not have been. She might have got a pep talk on resentment or rivalry, though probably not named as such. The words were too forceful. Certainly not jealousy; that was too sexual. Yvette considered herself a woman of the world, up for tackling most subjects. But nothing head on and not that one. Because she, Sylvie, had got in first, she had stopped it at source. Perhaps she was a strategist after all, though not a conscious one.

She replied, 'I haven't made plans to.'

'It would do you good to have a project.'

She means more children, Sylvie thought. As if

76

one thing were ever a substitute for another. In the days of heaven, they'd have been up there together, the ones who'd gone and the ones who were waiting to come down. Yvette made it clear that one baby was inadequate, scarcely more than none. Though, at the other end, more than three were too many. She herself had had two, Paul and his brother. The ideal number—though the brother had turned out less satisfactory than Paul. She had quizzed her daughter-in-law in the past about Eve's unproductiveness and her delay in production. It was a way of getting at Sylvie. Her reply that her parents had been happy, without anyone extra, had seemed whimsical.

'I don't really see going to London as a project. Is it?' she said.

'No, of course not, not like that. I'm sorry, I'm a few steps ahead, as usual. I've been thinking about how you might make life more interesting. You seem to look sad a lot of the time. We're worried about you.'

'Thank you.'

Her few steps ahead were an understatement. Yvette believed in short cuts. She always wanted to be there and back before she'd even set out.

'You might not take to the idea. It's only an idea. But let me try it out on you.'

She paused, as if Sylvie would find this enticing. Sylvie said nothing. Some phrases turned her off. This was one of them.

'You'll need to do something with the money from George's flat. There's no point leaving it sitting in a bank account.'

Sylvie saw herself, not the cash, in one of George's armchairs, trying to get comfortable;

77

something had happened to the upholstery. He hadn't bothered about such things. She and the chair were in the middle of a banking hall with people walking round her. They seemed not to notice her, but she was still in the way.

'So, how does that strike you, darling?'

'How does what strike me?'

'Sylvie, weren't you listening? I've been talking about the new annexe.'

'They aren't that old; just uncomfortable.'

'Old? Who's old, darling?'

Sylvie realised she had said it aloud. She hadn't meant to. She hadn't been listening either.

Yvette said, 'I was saying that conference facilities, even on a small scale, would give you and Paul such a boost.'

'You think so?'

'I really do.'

'It might take more than that.'

Yvette ignored this and said brightly, 'That's where the money is now.'

Sylvie considered. She didn't want to talk about this sort of thing out of doors. It made a false ceiling and took away the pleasure of being in the open. She could say that she already had enough to cope with. Lucien, Paul, Natalie, Maude, Felix, the guests who came and left. Keeping everyone calm but flowing was as much as she could manage. The idea of men and women in suits, with their names pinned on them, carrying packs like party bags, walking down a new long corridor, was oppressive to her. She could smell the fresh paint and the chip board. She could hear their footsteps and voices coming towards her. She stopped and listened. She wasn't prepared to let them come closer. There was

78

a path off to the left. From deep in it, beyond the point where it disappeared into the forest, she heard the whine of a saw.

'It isn't for sale, George's flat,' she said.

'I thought Paul said your father had left everything to you.'

Sylvie paused. She could invent another beneficiary—a woman for George. One who had lived with him. It was tempting. A few sentences and there she would be, useful for ever. A strong woman with a name. She would think of one in a moment, before they got to the next stack of timber. Like a dog with convincing teeth she would guard the flat in her absence. George could easily have met her in the last five years. It wouldn't have to be complicated, one of those relapses or revivals, depending how you told it. Nothing that detracted from Eve. People did just meet, didn't they? She warmed to the idea. Lies were usually denials; where I wasn't, who didn't exist, what hadn't happened. This was parsimonious—they were potentially more constructive. Children made things up from scratch. They didn't even need to be cornered. But this other woman was no more visible to her than George was. Sylvie could have put words together, nothing more. They wouldn't have been persuasive. Her mother, now that was different. She saw her leaning on the table looking George in the eye, argumentative but appreciative. She liked to engage with him. No one would ever have told Eve she needed a project. Her life was a project and George the best part of that.

'I don't want to talk about her,' she said.

'I understand,' said Yvette calmly.

'Paul's never said anything about building on. I

thought we'd had our share of that when we first came here,' Sylvie said.

'He dreams dreams,' said his mother.

'Perhaps we should turn round,' Sylvie said.

'It's something you could do together,' said Yvette. 'And it's something you could do for Paul.'

Sylvie ignored both parts of this sentence, not able to deal with either of them. She hadn't given any thought to what to do with the flat. The week in London had had her father's funeral in it; that had been enough. She had supposed she would sell it later when she was in a different frame of mind but that was as far as she'd got. It was something troublesome that had to be done, not an opportunity. She thought it strange how one thing could turn into another. Money had this inconsequentiality, this frivolous ability to bed down anywhere; it could pretend it was under your nose when it was really in Switzerland or a vault under the pavement. There was her father's inoffensive ground-floor flat with its foundations in London clay and its ceilings providing a floor for the person upstairs, the one who paced about in the early evening and occasionally played Mahler late at night. It was innocent of the designs on it; the metamorphosis into conference facilities.

Sylvie longed to get back. The walk, as a walk, wasn't working any more. She hated this happening. She couldn't stop it. One minute, whatever her thoughts, the outside outclassed her. The still air, the mist on the ground moving up through the trees. Even without feeling particular pleasure in what was around her, there was enough and to spare of it. Then, the next, it lost status; no more interesting than she was to herself.

80

'Please let's turn round,' she said.

'Are you tired, darling?'

'We were very late last night. Yes, I am. It's caught up with me.'

'Paul said there was going to be a big party. How did it go?'

'It was quite difficult, but we got through it.'

'That sounds rather negative. Was it so bad?'

'Paul will tell you about it, I expect.'

Sylvie began to walk faster. Yvette hurried beside her, anxious not to miss any part of the story Sylvie might let fall. At this stage of the walk, the extra speed made her catch her breath. She couldn't keep up and ask questions.

Sylvie knew there was some sort of cruelty in her behaviour. She knew because she didn't like to see this woman, older than herself, struggling. She kept looking ahead, in order not to see, but she wasn't oblivious to Yvette. She had to get from where they were now, to where she needed to be. It wasn't a question of place, though that came into it. It was more that she panicked about the transition, feared she would get stuck in it.

As they walked across the gravel towards the restaurant Sylvie heard herself saying, 'Do you want to come in and sit down for a minute before you drive back? We were out for quite a long time.'

Yvette immediately said that that was a nice idea, though she wasn't really tired, the exercise hadn't been especially strenuous. She was old enough to be proud of her mobility and liked to draw attention to it. So then Sylvie was stuck with her. She regretted the automatic politeness. It was all very well with the clients, but extended to family it encumbered her. Yvette said she would sit in the hall, she didn't want to get too settled. Sylvie was to get on with what she had to do. She sat on the arm of the armchair by the fire, to look provisional and less than elderly, and her daughter-in-law fetched her a glass of mineral water. Any type would do, she wasn't fussy.

Sylvie only wanted to do one thing. It wasn't administrative; nothing to do with the restaurant. She glanced at Yvette sipping water and turning the pages of a magazine. She wanted to think about the book and the blue envelope. There was no past attached to them, or only a few minutes' worth of conversation exchanged with their owner. And there wouldn't be a future. She wasn't that stupid.

She had trouble with daydreams, though. She was wary of them. They sprang up like night dreams, then she was stuck with them, until they had run their course. It was as if she put her hands on a ouija board and the words arranged themselves calmly, then, without warning, went haywire. They slipped over into reality and she had to extricate herself politely. Clients were strangers and they turned to her, needed looking after. Men, she was thinking of. At the end, there was nothing, there never had been anything, but it always left her feeling foolish and, somehow, resentful. For the time it lasted, and a little beyond, it changed things with Paul. She never knew why.

These objects were real, however, the book and the envelope. They weren't hers, or addressed to her, but she could do something with them; hide them away for comfort or use them like tickets to get somewhere.

The telephone rang. It was Maude. Yvette seemed to be close enough to hear both sides of the conversation. Perhaps she wasn't. Maude was saying she expected Sylvie had called the hospital.

'No I haven't. You have done, obviously.'

Yvette carried on flicking the pages but the pace altered.

Maude was re-running through the events of the previous evening and suddenly paused dramatically.

'I'm sorry,' Sylvie said.

She was saying that it had happened—there—in the restaurant.

'It happened *here*? What do you mean?'

Yvette was still.

Maude said, in a respectful whisper, that it had happened—there—before he got to hospital, before he was even taken away.

'Oh, I see. The precise moment *when.* I don't think that matters does it?'

Sylvie fitted the curls of the telephone wire round the index finger of her left hand. The voice carried on talking. The loops looked like exotic black rings on her finger, slightly menacing. She would never wear anything like that. Maude asked her if she was cross with her for talking about it. She said she hadn't meant to sound cross. Maude paused, then said Paul would want to be told what had happened.

'Yes, I'll tell him. Thank you for letting me know.'

Yvette glanced up, as if she expected Paul to walk in.

Sylvie thought, that must be the end, but it wasn't.

'Are you sending flowers?'

'I expect we will. I'll sort something out. I'll call the flower shop.'

83

'I wonder whether calling is special enough? They might not give it their full attention.'

'Well, yes, I suppose I could go round there in person, but it's not really necessary. I know the woman there. She'll tell me what she's got that's decent.'

Maude calmed down and then started up again. 'Sylvie. There will have to be a message. You mustn't leave it to the florist.'

'Of course I won't leave it to her. I'll tell her what to put.'

Maude talked rapidly and quietly and seemed to end up saying something not quite clear. Her name.

'*Your* name? Sorry I don't understand.'

Added.

'Added to what?'

Yvette took another sip of water.

She was telling her what to write. Paul, Sylvie, Maude. She showed some restraint in the order.

'I see. I'd have thought something more general. But that's all right. I'll do that.'

'I did know Maurice,' she said. 'I'm not trying to be pushy.'

'No, it's all right. I said so. I'll do it. It's fine.'

'Is it really all right?'

'Really.'

'You'll tell Paul, won't you?'

'Yes, I shall. Bye.'

Sylvie put the telephone down and switched on the computer.

'That was Maude,' she said.

She need not have said anything. But the person she had been speaking to and the person in the room had met. She had no idea what they thought

84

of each other, though she guessed that there was admiration there somewhere. It would have been unnatural to keep silent. Yvette left the magazine open as if she might continue with it. She looked at once blithe and sympathetic.

'Is everything all right, darling?'

'Maude told me that Maurice—that's the man we were giving the retirement party for yesterday evening—he died.'

'That's terrible. When did that happen?'

'Last night. He collapsed.'

'Here? You don't mean here, darling?'

'Yes.'

'Where?'

Sylvie said nothing.

'In the dining room? Not at the table?'

Still nothing.

'Darling, why didn't you tell me? Such a shock for you. A dreadful shock.' She paused and thought. 'You said it had been a difficult evening. I'd no idea it was anything like this. Why didn't you tell me?'

'I don't know really. I didn't feel like talking about it.'

Yvette looked at her, didn't get up. She was about to say something and thought better of it. She heard Sylvie's reply in advance from across the room, though neither of them spoke. Faint and cross it was going to be. Brought what all back? What's *he* got to do with it? So Yvette never mentioned George after all.

*   *   *

Sylvie knew that her mother-in-law was hurt that

85

she had failed to confide in her about Maurice, but she ignored the grievance and got on with composing the note to accompany the flowers. She did it in her head. A formula was best, simple and unsentimental with their names at the end, Maude's by request. She would avoid naming the restaurant; macabre publicity at the graveside. If they didn't know who they were from, that was just too bad. She had read the messages that people had sent with George's funeral flowers. They were all different: some to him, some for or about him, some misspelled by the florist. Don had advised her against. He had told her to say Family Flowers Only. But this seemed hard on the friends and the flowers—and left the family, which was really just her, rather exposed.

She took advantage of her efficiency with the note, made it carry over into writing the letter to the Englishman. So that ended up straightforward too. She wrote it as soon as Yvette left. She said he'd left his book behind. She'd quite like to read it, if that was all right, before sending it back, but if he wanted it sooner she'd post it. None of the strange, almost spellbound feelings she'd had about finding it got into her letter, which was a good thing or he never would have replied. She realised that and also realised that it was just luck that they didn't.

CHAPTER NINE

Jerry Dorney slit open her letter with the knife he'd used to butter his toast. He had left his plate on the window sill and gone down three floors of common parts as soon as he'd noticed the postman's trolley on the pavement below. He hadn't come to terms with the trolley. He could still run up and down the stairs, even if the fellow couldn't heave a bit of mail. It was a habit from school days, rushing to the post. Rigmaroles from his Ma and his Aunt Lou, it used to be, an antiphonal chant, one week on, one week off. The second post of the day he always threw straight in the bin unopened. It wasn't worth bothering with; begging letters and mail order.

He had no idea who Sylvie Delacour was. Sylvie. His mind was a blank. He gave up.

On his way to work, about half an hour later, driving through London traffic, he almost ran a woman over. She just stepped out. He leant on his horn and she stopped. She didn't move, she stood in the road. The way her ankles were neatly lined up, the expression on her face, neither quite right in the circumstances, brought back another woman. Someone who had just stood there not far away from him. He remembered her. No, that's too strong. He was able to remember something about her.

The address at the top of the letter now made sense. He'd been trying to recall when he'd last taken a woman to a hotel.

*   *   *

He had gone to the house in the Vosges to catch up and he probably would have done if he hadn't kept falling asleep. What catching up meant he hadn't defined properly, though he had used the phrase to himself. He had felt cheerful about going there, free of responsibility. It was the family holiday house, though they usually ended up taking their holidays somewhere else; paying twice over, in fact. He stacked up piles of paper and documents into a couple of old cardboard wine boxes with the slats taken out, put them in the boot of the car and brought them with him. They didn't lie neatly, as they were destabilised by slithery plastic covers and smaller fatter objects such as the calculator and the bundle of envelopes from the tax office. He was easy about it, he could put up with a certain amount of confusion.

The place was so quiet. He had never been there on his own and had imagined it would be the same as being there with Gillian and the children, only more peaceful, as if removing talk and disturbance left things neutral.

He lined up half a dozen bottles on the wide shelf in the kitchen, shoved the contents of a plastic bag into the fridge, turned the dial on the electric boiler from nought to five, while holding down the red button. He lit a fire with half a firelighter and some kindling and logs he'd bought in a garage. Nothing went too badly wrong and he felt quite active. He thought he would impose himself on the silence and the dark dampness. A couple of hours passed and it still hadn't happened. He put on an extra jersey. Stepping on a particular floorboard set up vibrations that made the cutlery in the drawer jingle, but after a while he didn't need to walk about. He spread out the papers he'd brought from home on the table and sat down in front of them. He got up to look for a pen and, when he couldn't find one, he retrieved the morning's newspaper from the log basket. He sat down again. He'd already read it pretty thoroughly in the Tunnel. The fire was getting going, taking out the oxygen. Within five minutes he was asleep, his head at an awkward angle on his arms.

That night he gave in to it, let the house have its own way. He plunged into a deep well. Not just into sleep, but somewhere down among the tree roots. When daylight came he got out of bed, but he never resurfaced. He went to the bar in the village to call his wife and his secretary. They both asked how he was and whether he'd had a good journey, but neither seemed to have any sense of how far away he was. They talked to him as if he were in Berkshire. It's bloody freezing, he said, but this didn't give much idea of the cold quiet fog, breached by hooting and church bells, or the men, with ice on their boots and caps on their heads, laying claim to the first beer of the morning. Both women wanted, since he was on the line, to check a few dates. He could see them. Norma sitting in a sort of box in the office, like an island or a pew, with only her head and shoulders showing, leafing through his diary, licking her index finger to get a purchase on the pages. Gillian, at home, reading the wall calendar, stepping back from it because she couldn't find her reading glasses. Odd things it had printed on it, like Thanksgiving and the feast of the Immaculate Conception, that the family took no notice of. He disliked his diary, the way it got spattered on months ahead. For years it had been blank with only the coming week inked over. That was when he'd been in control of it. Now they sorted out his arrangements between them, Norma and Gillian, and he appeared in the right places like the Holy Ghost after the Ascension. That had been on the calendar too, though he couldn't remember when. Aunt Lou would know, or would have done before her mind furred up. There was no way of stopping it, any of it. Exorcism, something drastic.

* * *

He stayed a couple more nights in the house. A cloud settled on the mountain; there was no variation in the weather and not much in the level of light. He had trouble distinguishing one hour from another. He was tired, even after so much sleeping. It was only after he was back on the road that he started to come to. He got off the spiralling mountain track and onto the wider route with cars flicking past on the other carriageway. The air from the vents cleared his head and the cloud turned to rain. He couldn't remember much about the past few days. He listened to opera as he drove; nothing too heavy, or early or recent. Then a burst of something from the sixties. It was good to be moving. He liked the sensation of putting miles under the wheels, checking the distances against the clock. The mental arithmetic, speed–time–distance thing, sharpened him up. If he kept going, got on the motorway, whipped past the slag-heaps, industrial towns and brief views of cathedrals, he'd be in Calais in no time, and in England by early evening. Scratch supper with Gillian, or, if he got stuck in traffic, take-away, in West London. He noticed the sign on the roof of the restaurant, off the main road, clear of the trees, loopy letters outlined in metal. He wouldn't, at that time of day, have known they were blue. They weren't lit up, but it was Paul and Sylvie's restaurant.

*   *   *

A woman found a key from the board behind the desk and showed him upstairs. She went ahead and turned down the passage when she got to the top. The stairs were at one end, so there was no choice as to which way to go. She didn't waste a gesture on it. The level of lighting was low; economical, not sexy. There were prints on the walls, some sort of series of fruit. They broke up the surface. She opened a door. The curtains inside the room were half drawn. She had gone out quietly. He had called his wife and stretched out on the bed, dozed for a while.

Downstairs, at dinner, the dining room was livelier than he'd expected. He had had a foaming bath and washed his hair and felt a bit brighter. He took in the glint in the wine glasses and the clean white linen. No local artists' oil paintings or stuffed magpies. These places could be dire, unless you had a taste for noting minute degrees of deadness. His Aunt Lou had gone in for that, describing in detail the visiting ministers who came to preach in the month of August, or the skirts in Marks and Spencer. She got a lot out of life, relishing the dreary. She used to say that the bridge with the station and the shops on, over the railway lines at

West Hampstead, reminded her of the Ponte Vecchio. He took a book to the table, though not with any intention of reading. It was protection. You never knew who might not try to strike up conversation. Some fellow telling you his weekly sales or recounting First World War history, having had a fascinating time visiting battlefields and war graves. What a waste. He agreed. And if the other person said that he couldn't help thinking the best had perished, he agreed with that too. You only had to look around you.

On the other side of the room was a long table laid for a party. Next to him, a couple who seemed to be talking to each other. They wouldn't bother him. He found himself staring at the objects in front of him. Knife, fork, glass, big and small of each, an overlarge plate they'd whip away again, a napkin, a vase with a flower in that his wife would have been able to identify. One of everything. He hadn't been particular, on his own in the Vosges. He'd washed up before he'd left, though, and checked there was nothing left in the fridge.

*   *   *

It hadn't been the cold, or the damp, or the loneliness that had done for him, it had been being there. He recognised the condition. When he got to wherever he was going, arriving at any of his three houses, the buoyancy left him. Parking, stopping, turning off the engine, the sudden quiet inside the car, whatever the noise outside; each stage left him lower. It had happened enough times; a kind of agoraphobia at getting out of the car and a kind of claustrophobia at going indoors. He couldn't

92

explain it. They weren't houses bearing weight from the past, passing on family defects. Each had been bought in the usual way with borrowed money and a certain amount of arm-twisting from other people. It was true that they all had something pretty serious wrong with them. None was reliably saleable, which worried him whenever he set foot in them, though in between, particularly in transit, he could contemplate them calmly, think of them as assets. Driving fast, he had been able to picture them, as if they were odd roadside buildings that he passed and discounted.

There was the London flat in a house, with a front, ugly and chaotic enough to be the back; brick, not stucco and with too many drainpipes slithering down the walls. It was on a main road; that's how you knew which way round it was. Then there was the one with its feet in some tributary of the Thames, that his wife saw as solid. Then there was the Vosges. They had flashed by, his houses, interruptions in long stretches of forest, bare winter fields, patches of vineyard.

*   *   *

Gillian took their properties and finances for granted. She didn't question him. She never had done. That's why he'd chosen her. The others up till then had wanted clarification. He remembered the word because they'd used it. He had supposed, then, that they knew what they meant by it. Not, do you love me, or will you always love me, but, I think we should clarify our relationship. Leaning against a door, or against him, looking straight at him or looking away, bold down the telephone, or

93

hesitant. Something about him had made them ask for it. And later, once he was married, the ones who from time to time participated in his expense account, had been even more insistent, not even bothering to lean. What a word. Clarification. He hadn't liked it. Different again from clarity or shedding light. Not that he had come up with those, nor had Gillian. The fluidity that he'd seen as promising, had been more like absence or absentmindedness, and in bed the same; she hadn't been adaptable, just not quite with it. They had started buying. Houses and what went inside them. The flurry of getting and spending warmed them up for a time, every time. But the feeling went and wasn't replaced by another. Just a lack. At least the money built up again slowly. They had the things though. Three sets of everything. If you piled up all the plates they'd hit the ceiling. No, scrape against it: nothing dramatic.

* * *

Jerry said he would have what was on offer for dinner. The choice of the chef. And a decent bottle. He let the woman choose. He didn't even open the wine list. It wasn't so much that he couldn't make a decision, as that the process of decision-making had dissolved. He began to see that it had always been a put-up job; a check list written on one of those magic note pads children used to play with. You pulled back the filmy top sheet and it all disappeared. Take the purchase of the house in the Vosges he'd just been to. A few years before he had been in Basle on one of his regular trips. Someone in the office was passing round photographs of the cottage he wanted to sell. Jerry thought there would be no harm in looking, so he and the colleague went to see it, after an Alsatian lunch. The colleague had driven fairly fast, considering the lunch and the gradient. They arrived at this dead end, silent and green, smelling of forest. The difference between the picture and the real place was compelling, more so than usual. He had thought, for some reason, of Norwegian Wood, though Gillian didn't and never had resembled the girl in that song. He had never slept in the bath either. Falling asleep in it, as he had done last night and the night before, didn't count.

*   *   *

It's very isolated. It's very dark. His wife's voice had sounded, although the sentences were short, as if she were exploring difficult concepts. It was the first time he had taken her there. She walked round the rooms, looking as she looked when she walked round rooms at home in England, or National Trust houses. She was too tall for the place, too resistant, physically inappropriate. He couldn't help feeling it, though he knew it was unreasonable. She was as she was. Transformation was out of the question. She was the same out of doors, in the plot that surrounded the house. It wasn't a garden, though you wouldn't have known from the way she paced about; her feet labouring through the wet thick-stemmed grass, as if Barry, who came every Thursday from April to October to the house in the Thames valley, had failed to give it a proper mow. She glanced up at the fir trees, surprised to see them there.

In a sense she rose to the occasion. She didn't say much, but she sorted things out with a cloth in her hand, mopping up excess moisture wherever she found it. They made up the bed in silence.

She talked more at dinner. She talked about their daughter, how she got on the wrong side of the teachers, or one particular one. And their son's homework. And Aunt Lou, how much longer she could cope on her own, what strange things she'd said when she last came to stay. These topics evolved over time, without changing. They might just as well have been at home in England. He could see them now. The bulb over the table casting a circle of light. Within the circle, an open bottle, half a loaf, wine glasses and the far rim of their plates; outside it, the rest of the table and the two of them in near darkness. He remembered someone telling him that the bit of Omar Khayyam, that everybody knew, included a leg of lamb in the original. He couldn't really see his wife's face, but she carried on talking. He didn't mention Omar Khayyam. It had been one of those pointlessly long summer evenings. Twilight indoors.

The next day they'd gone shopping. He had driven into Strasbourg and parked in an underground car park. They had bought the house furnished, from the colleague in Basle, but they still needed to buy things. They had gone round together to find them. It had been quite an agreeable day, with lunch in the middle. Whenever he stayed he was aware that there were objects that didn't fit in; the bread bin and the bedside lamps. There were others. They never stopped looking imported, which was funny given they had been bought locally. That was their last house purchase.

96

It hadn't done anything for them.

*   *   *

When Maurice slumped in his chair, Jerry Dorney knew it could have been him. Because that was how it would probably happen. He would be thinking of something quite different, not even present in his surroundings. Taken not from life but from a place in his head. Was that nearer or further?

*   *   *

He did remember something of Sylvie. She seemed to him like those arrangements of poplars that you see when you're driving through France. Very formal, on the diagonal, but something about the formality making you see the oddness of trees, their particular strangeness. As a person, she wasn't clearly defined, but then neither was he at that moment.

CHAPTER TEN

He wasn't sorry to have lost his copy of *The Egoist*. His daughter had given it to him for his fifty-first birthday because she said she thought it was something to do with that magazine he read all weekend. He said that that was *The Spectator*. He was pretty sure she knew this and that someone had drawn her attention to the title, a teacher who'd read more than *Animal Farm*, if there were such a person. She had probably told whoever was on the till at the book shop that she was buying it for her father. Alice was like that. Sylvie, yes he called her that, not Sylvie Delacour or Madame Delacour, should, therefore, keep it for as long as she wanted. Actually, as it was a reproach to him, he would be glad if she kept it for ever. He wasn't much of a fiction reader, not of that kind of thing, anyway. He liked to imagine it living a blameless existence in the valley of the Meuse. He signed himself Jerry. And Yours.

*   *   *

That was all, really. But, Sylvie thought, it was quite a lot as a reply to a woman who had poured his wine, swiped his credit card and written him one short letter. Otherwise, the asymmetry was still all the other way. He knew more about her than she knew about him. Like all the clients he would have a view of her, a view contained in a fixed frame; nothing arbitrary about where it began and ended.

98

She was sitting in a bar in the nearby town, the only customer at a table, the only woman in the place. Jerry's letter was open in front of her. It didn't fit with the man in her mind. She tried to piece him together, Jerry, her correspondent, the bits of his face. It took some doing. She remembered remembering people complete, developing them in her mind's eye, like photographs from Instamatic cameras. This man came in parts and the more she concentrated the less she saw. She got glimpses of his eyes, more than one expression in them, and something of the width of his face and the contours of his chin, but his mouth not at all. What she'd liked about him straight away was his look of mild dismay, as if life wasn't turning out as expected.

The postman had turned up as usual about an hour before and put the bundle of envelopes on her desk without looking at her. It had been like that since they'd misunderstood each other. A clean decision to throw them on the mat would have been better. Half measures made both of them uncomfortable. She had known it was from him. She had opened it and read it quickly. Everything about it was astonishing. She remembered his voice as if he were there. She had liked his voice. The handwriting and the voice didn't fit together straight away. Then they did. She hadn't imagined his reply; that would have been madness. She might never have got a reply at all. Yet, she must have imagined something, or how could these words in front of her seem so different? She had put the letter in her bag, gone out to the car, put the bag on the seat next to her. She glanced at it from time to time as she was driving, as if it were someone she had impetuously offered a lift to and was now nervous of.

*   *   *

She had parked easily. There weren't many people about. She had avoided the short stretch of shops licked by prosperity, the florist, the hairdresser and the salon de thé she sometimes went to afterwards, to recover from spending too long in front of a mirror. She had walked in the opposite direction, past premises boarded up, or struggling to keep going. The Bar des Sports was in a wedge between two streets, with windows facing both sides. It was narrow at the entrance and broadened towards the bar and the half-curtained-off stairs that went down to the telephones and toilets. The arrangement was the opposite of perspective and seemed to remove the choice of forward motion. It suited her to be here. Compared with the café near George's flat, where she had gone for breakfast in the week of his funeral, this place was stuck in the past, unimproved. No one fussed about cigarette ash and rings left by red wine and coffee. The windows were bleary with old condensation. Looking in, or looking out through them, shapes were hazy, blocks of smudged colour, occasionally moving. Sylvie was glad to have found somewhere that preserved life at a time she felt nostalgia for. The bars she had hung around in with her school friends had been like this. Walls like scorched ironing board covers, the pattern breaking through in patches, and darkening towards the ceiling. The fan hanging from the middle, coated in greasy dust. The lighting over-yellowed and unflattering. She recognised the music, and—in general terms—the owner, who had that profound pissed-off look that was to do with the decade he was young in, nothing to do with his age.

He had ignored her when she walked in. She had sat and waited, then gone up to the counter to order her coffee and carry it back to her table. Now he got himself from his side of the bar to hers. Everything was an effort, but an insouciant effort. He affected a limp. He took away her cup and asked her if she wanted another. He walked across to the door, the cup still in one hand, and shut it properly, so that the draught and the voices outside stopped and the glass had a chance to steam up. This was a man who liked fug. She felt she understood him. It had happened before with men she just came across. No type in particular; the selection was random. They didn't have to say anything. She had a friend, Adrienne, whom she'd known from their schooldays, who used to talk about boys and men smiling at her. She always got them into the conversation, these special smiles. Sylvie didn't think her feeling was the same. She hoped it didn't come from vanity. It seemed not to come from inside at all. It was more as if she were in a wide open space, insanely open, and saw someone else in it; not anyone special, no one just for her, but there was recognition.

She took out Jerry's letter again. She could sense the man watching her; not critical, or nosy, or sexually interested, even. She felt secure, as if she had two men after her, and she had the luxury of choosing between them. It was restful knowing he was looking. She couldn't remember Paul looking at her in that way, without meaning anything, as if she was a good place to lay his eyes. She hadn't realised when she was young that this was something she wanted. She didn't blame herself. How could she have known in advance?

*   *   *

She had been in a telephone booth in the Gare de l'Est calling her mother. She had promised she would tell her she had arrived in Paris, though it annoyed her to have to; shut up with the smell of old coins and smoke. She was twenty. An old man opened the door and grinned, slowly moving the short distance towards her. The station noises burst in, then the door shut behind him. She gave him a shove, without taking her eyes off his face, and he was out again, still grinning, walking backwards and waving. It was one of those encounters that disorder the lives of girls and women. The worst thing was explaining to Eve why she had stopped in mid sentence and sounded out of breath and distracted when she started talking again. Eve never let anything go by unexplained.

The weekend wasn't memorable. She had sat about in a tiny room with Adrienne, who had complained of dry skin and the moral philosophy teacher and rubbed cream into her knees. They had only gone out once it got dark. They both cheered up, walking along, though they told each other they had no interest in this party they were going to. They had been careful not to dress up; simply unravelled themselves from the knots they were in on the floor and took it in turns to draw swift, accurate black lines round their eyes in front of the mirror. She met Paul at the party. He said he didn't recognise anyone. He might even be in the wrong place. He'd been told the party was in this block and that the door would be open and he had walked through the first that he saw. Well, you wouldn't expect random people to leave their doors open would you? But the music didn't sound quite right; it was loud enough, but symphonic, a full symphony orchestra. He'd followed the sound into the only room with a light on and there was a man on his own, with a glass of beer in his hand and a small bowl of shrimps on the table. With their shells on, Sylvie asked, or sitting in a pool of pink water. Shells on Paul said. Did he offer you one, Sylvie asked. No, Paul said, he just looked really disappointed. I expect she turned up soon, Sylvie said. Paul laughed and said he was glad she was optimistic. He asked her her name and she told him. He was fed up with meeting depressed girls. They were all depressed where he came from. And none of them bothered about food. He was really glad she was interested in shrimps.

Sylvie made him repeat the name of the place three times through the noise. She was sorry to meet someone local. That wasn't the point of coming to Paris. And in any case he wasn't the type she usually fancied. She edged her way past some immovable boys to get herself a drink. Adrienne, who knew the girls who were giving the party, ignored her; too preoccupied with the special smiles that were flashed at her. Sylvie swallowed a plastic cup full of wine and smoked a cigarette. No one else spoke to her. She would have hung over the balcony but it was already overloaded and six floors up from a courtyard. In the middle of the room, where there might have been dancing, someone was sobbing and at least four people had their arms round her. Sylvie made for the door. Paul intercepted her and asked her if anything was the matter. He called her Sylvie. She said she'd had enough and he followed her down the stairs. She took no notice of him, but she didn't mind his being behind her. When she got to the bottom, she didn't recognise the street or remember how she and Adrienne had got there. She crossed over and started walking. She supposed she'd find her way. Paul caught up and walked beside her. He asked her one or two questions that didn't lead anywhere. The conversation kept faltering. He seemed less sure of himself than he had done upstairs. And although in one way Sylvie liked him for this, in another she felt more uncomfortable. It left her exposed and she had to deal with the silences. He didn't pretend he knew Paris, but he had a better sense of direction than she had and got her to a bridge that she recognised. They stood on the corner by a flight of stone steps that went down to the river. She wouldn't let him walk her any further. They were facing each other, and he might have looked at her, in the way she later found out she wanted to be looked at, but he didn't. They found out that they had both caught a train from Metz, which was hardly a coincidence as they lived within ten miles of each other. They didn't pretend it was one. She told him about the man in the telephone box. She didn't make it sound worse than it had been. He looked angry with the man as if it had just happened, and protective towards her. She hadn't quite bargained for that, so soon after his uncertainty, but she was relieved to have found something real to talk about.

Her mother had met George in Verdun. She was wearing a scarlet skirt that had got caught on the spike of some low railings by the Episcopal Palace. She had gone down the steps from the park with her cousin, Charlotte, and bought scarlet thread and a needle. The shop assistant had been sniffy that Eve didn't have a needle on her. Extensive mending was still expected in the fifties. Women couldn't assume they were modern and choose to give up on it. The girls climbed back up and found a bench where Eve could sit and stitch the skirt up again. She had made it herself so she knew which colour to ask for in the haberdasher's; it was an exact match. She didn't know how she'd manage without taking it off, but there was plenty of cloth in it and she swivelled it round and turned the torn part wrong side out without showing too much stocking. She took a sliver out of the hem as a patch. George and his friend were taking an afternoon off from investigating the Great War battlefield to the north of the city. This was serious study after National Service. They picked the girls up, two pretty French girls. Eve was always happy to see herself through the eyes of an appreciative male. It made her seem old fashioned and unintellectual; charming, in a way. The young men waited while Eve finished off her sewing. They stood up and the girls were seated. Then they took them to a café for ices and chicory coffee. George had been the good-looking one and not necessarily English. They, the other pair had had to manage as best they could. Not terribly well, in fact. He, wasn't he called Colin, sweetheart, that pedantic friend of yours, had said that it wouldn't have happened in London, as all the railings had gone for the war effort. The cousin, Charlotte, had taken offence. Eve couldn't blame her, though she wasn't really listening, taken up as she was by George. In Verdun of all places to say such a thing. With all those losses. Which war they'd occurred in was irrelevant. Afterwards they walked by the river. There was so much she wanted to tell him, but of course, although his French was not bad, she had to speak more slowly than usual. This steadied her up, which was a good thing, as she was rather breathless at having met him at all.

When he left, she felt so lonely. It was awful saying goodbye to him. Although Charlotte stayed for another week, and they were good friends, it made no difference. She had never felt lonely in her life until then. He and his friend had had an itinerary that took them to Nancy for an earlier slice of history. He came back again on his way to England, though this wasn't part of the original plan and his friend was annoyed. And, when he left, she had had to say goodbye all over again and then she felt even lonelier, worse than before. She kept the needle with the few centimetres of scarlet thread in it. She tied knots at both ends.

* * *

This was the fixed story. It never altered. Eve was sure about love. She didn't mind talking about it, as part of her narration, or asking her daughter if she was convinced she was in it. This she did insistently in the time between Sylvie saying she and Paul might be marrying and the marriage. She knew better than to call it an engagement. No one called it that any more, her daughter told her.

Sylvie grew up associating love with a kind of certainty and precision that made her uncomfortable. Her mother seemed to her naïve; a product of her time. Those post-war emotions were high definition, edged with euphoria from pulling together. She and George had been young in the war, but they were marked by it. In a way, Sylvie envied her but she couldn't get back there; it seemed like regression. She could have changed endlessly the account of her meeting with Paul. It was hardly worth telling. So what was the difference? That she wasn't interested in the essence of it, or that she was cleverer than her mother, or that her mother had a daughter to tell the story to? Her mother and father had stayed loving each other. Perhaps that was what fixed it.

*   *   *

She told the man behind the bar she had changed her mind. She would have another cup of coffee. He told her to sit down again. He'd bring it to her. The two men drinking beer at the bar both turned round briefly and stared at her, then carried on their conversation.

CHAPTER ELEVEN

'I didn't think anyone would miss me.'

Paul was waiting in the hall for her. It was a quarter past eleven and well short of lunch-time.

'*Did* anyone miss me?'

'Where were you?'

'Nowhere in particular.'

'You took the car, so you must have been somewhere.'

Sylvie shook her head. She wondered how long they could talk about places without naming them.

'Do you really not know where you were, or are you pretending?'

He had started off looking parental; both worried and threatening. This was when she first walked in. She hadn't felt threatened but she had noticed and had to stop herself from flicking her head in a sod-that gesture, re-learned from the proprietor of the café. Jacques, he was called. Her hands relaxed at her sides, more complacent, not needing restraint. Odd how different parts of the body took on different roles.

'I went into town and sat in a bar, the Bar des Sports,' Sylvie said. 'It wasn't particularly agreeable. Actually, I wouldn't recommend it. But I was quite happy sitting there. I drank two cups of coffee which I paid for. Then the owner gave me another one and a glass of red wine. And a cigarette. He said he'd stopped doing boiled eggs. He boiled them and threw them away for weeks, before it occurred to him to give up on it. No one missed them. He still had the metal thing. You know, the thing they fit in, they're quite neat. He asked me what else he might put in it.'

'I'm sure you were full of bright ideas.'

'I was, as it happens.'

'So, what else?'

'Don't you want to know what they were?'

'Not especially.'

'He asked me if I knew the Belgian seaside. He thought it might be my kind of place. He said we should have a day out at le Coq sur Mer. Now I think about it, I'm not sure it has sur Mer on the end. It sort of went with the eggs. It was nice of him wasn't it?'

'Very.'

A woman in a heavy mac and an efficient weatherproof hat came in through the main entrance.

'Good morning,' said Sylvie.

'We're not stopping for lunch,' the woman said. She started to climb the stairs.

'That's fine,' said Sylvie. 'We'll look forward to seeing you at dinner.'

A man opened the front door. It had only just shut, slowed down unnaturally by the fire prevention mechanism. He nodded at them both without looking at them. He used the stair rail hand over hand. Sylvie heard a key turning upstairs and a door opening and closing. The man was still only half way up.

'They won't be stopping for anything else either.'

'Sylvie,' Paul said, 'he'll hear you.'

'No he won't,' said Sylvie.

She thought, once he would have smiled and now he was disapproving, and not because of her carelessness with the clients, but because they themselves were as far from going to bed in the middle of the day as this creaking pair.

'He won't know what I'm talking about. They must have taken their key out with them,' she said.

'You weren't here when they left.'

'They could have hung it up for themselves. Stupid to carry it round. It's so heavy.'

'Sylvie, I think we need to talk.'

'Fine.'

'Here's not the best place. We could go back home but there are things I need to do in the kitchen.' He always called their rooms home.

Sylvie shrugged her shoulders 'I'd rather get it over with.'

She followed him into the kitchen. It was a good place for an interrogation, she thought; the metal and the echoes and the smooth surfaces. Not unlike the dentist's, but it was cosier at the dentist's and there was always a chance of anaesthetic. The lights were full on overhead, very bright.

Paul didn't speak, or even give her a warning look. Lucien was eating biscuits, perched on a stool. There was nowhere for his knees to go, crammed against the side of a work block and, even though he had his back to her, Sylvie could see he was uncomfortable. He didn't turn round. Paul didn't look at her either. She wanted to say, why didn't you tell me he'd been sent home from school and give me the chance to be an ordinary mother. Her rudeness to Paul, just now, her account of Jacques' offer, seemed merely silly. Water was running over a pile of green leaves in one of the sinks. It hit them at an angle and splashed up and back down again, but not tidily. A subsidiary fountain was spraying the floor. Paul and Lucien

110

were both ignoring it. Sylvie crossed the room and turned off the tap. It was suddenly quiet, apart from a few remaining drips and the continuous breathing sound of the oven. She went over to Lucien and put her arm round him.

'What are you doing back home?' she said.

He didn't reply. Sylvie looked at Paul.

'What's been happening?' she said.

'The school secretary called me and said Lucien had a stomach ache and thought he was going to throw up.'

'Did you?' she asked Lucien.

'I went to collect him,' Paul said. 'He wondered where you were. Obviously he expected you would go for him. I told him you would be here when we got back. But you weren't.'

'You're feeling better, now, though, are you?'

Lucien didn't speak. He prodded his middle, then nodded without looking at her.

'It's nearly lunch-time, sweet. You come and sit at my desk in the hall and run and tell me if anyone comes in. Will you do that? I need to come back and talk to Paul for a few minutes.'

He didn't agree but he got down from the stool and took her hand when she held it out.

When she got back to the kitchen, Paul wasn't there. She waited.

*   *   *

There were various framed certificates on the wall and a photograph of Paul. He was smiling, in his regalia, and looking relaxed by a table of food. There was a silver cup twinkling behind him. He had wanted to hold it but Sylvie had said it would

111

look better on the shelf above his left shoulder. An identical photograph hung in the hall. It had caused a few problems. Paul had wanted to get the team to stand in a line, with him in the middle, like God the Father. To be fair, he hadn't actually said he would be in the middle, but the chef always was in these cases. If the number was even, they wheeled on an extra, the gardener or someone. The result would be hung in the hall or the dining room. Sylvie had been scandalised. It showed in her face before she could stop it. She knew, because his face reflected it back to her, not the same look, but the extremity of it. Paul couldn't understand what was wrong, became very defensive. She had said that there weren't enough of them, they would look silly. It would be like a classroom photo in which half the children were off school with chickenpox. He took it badly; made out that she was suggesting he hadn't made it, got a big enough establishment. He had backed into this hole before, though he didn't like being there and she could honestly say she didn't recognise it as anywhere she had put him. The whole thing was stupid. Somewhere there was a parallel argument going on with a different opening, the one she hadn't been able to use because it was too complicated. That she wouldn't be able to bear seeing them standing there, smiling and trapped, lined up eternally—she, herself, looking aberrant, less photogenic than Maude. So she had been sad on two counts; that they weren't having the row they should have been having and that they were going through the moves of a pointless one. She had mentioned the photo to George in a letter; made a joke of it. She hadn't written about the argument.

She heard Paul's shoes on the floor behind her. He touched her arm above the elbow. Sylvie turned round immediately. She saw his expression. He looked as if he was making an effort. To think or to keep control, she wasn't sure which. She wished then that she hadn't turned round, that she had closed her eyes and rested against him. They could both have rested. Now they were straight back where they left off. She could hear it in her voice, but she couldn't stop it.

'I shouldn't think I'll go,' she said. 'You don't need to worry. It was a nice thought, that was all.'

'That isn't what I meant. I'm not worried about that.'

'Le Coq?'

'No.'

'That's a shame. What, then?' she said.

'I hoped that as things settled down you'd get back to normal,' he said.

'You make it sound perfect.'

'Make what sound perfect?'

'Normality.'

As though it were a place that you were flung from and to which you gratefully crept back after a moderate length of time. With any luck you wouldn't be flung too often in a lifetime. But she didn't speak because she knew she was repelled by the phrases he was using and that this was unreasonable. He wanted to help her and she wanted help, though not this sort. He wouldn't understand if she told him. She herself wouldn't have understood a month ago. Then she was

113

approaching death a step at a time. It was a progression, not entirely uncomfortable, seemingly adult and accepting. She wasn't aware that this was what she had thought, until it had gone. Now she couldn't get back there. This thing that was her life, and that took up so much time and all her energy, was a box she moved around in. She tapped the sides and looked in corners, and outside death was stretching out for ever, in every direction.

'I wonder if you should go and talk to someone,' Paul said.

There was no point in pretending she didn't know what sort of person he had in mind.

'What makes you say that?'

'You're so odd, Sylvie.'

She didn't reply. She could put up with being odd and his thinking her so, but she couldn't bear that he should divide the oddness up piecemeal and tell her about it.

'Don't say any more. Please.'

'All right. Not if you don't want me to.'

'Thank you.'

'Promise me you'll give it some thought, though. Will you?'

As if she ever stopped thinking.

'It's not just me who's worried. Other people. My mother. She was really disturbed by you the other day.'

'Your mother. What was she on about?' This she could cope with. 'I just couldn't be bothered to go into it all. Surely you understand that. She'd have wanted all the details.'

'What are you talking about, Sylvie?'

'Maurice and the heart attack. I simply didn't want to talk about it.'

114

'I didn't mean that.'

'What did you mean, then?'

'Telling her your father had a woman living with him.'

'I didn't tell her.'

'Suggesting, then.'

'Well, he might have done. It's not so implausible. I wish he had done. For his sake.'

'But he didn't. You know he didn't.'

Sylvie said nothing.

He looked at her. 'You do make things up. I don't know if you know you're doing it. Did you make it up about the man in the bar? You haven't had a cigarette in years.'

Sylvie still said nothing. She walked away from him and stopped by a large copper bowl. She saw herself in it, glinting and distorted; her mouth stretched beyond endurance across her face. She turned it the right way up.

'How's Maude?' she said.

'You know as well as I do,' he said. 'She was here at the weekend. Don't start on that.'

'All right. If you say not.' She smiled.

'Sylvie. You have no cause to be jealous.'

'No? I don't know that I am. Not jealous. That's not the right word. It's hard to explain.'

She always did this, got caught up on accuracy and lost him, lost herself on some point of definition. She should have gone back to the beginning, to the time when they seemed to be together. Eve had said she mustn't put up with second best, which had annoyed her. Women like her mother needed to be, or to pretend to be, passionately in love to have sex at all. They didn't seem to realise how nice it was anyway. Sylvie had

115

felt worldly and clear sighted.

'Are you going to try to explain?' Paul said.

She couldn't start from the beginning. This thing with Maude was a ragged fingernail, at the far end of a limb nearly detached from a body; capable of causing pain, but nerveless. She couldn't bear to re-connect it.

'I read something that made sense to me about it. I can't remember exactly. I could go and get the book.'

She left abruptly; walked back through the dining room and into the hall. Lucien wasn't there, though her chair was askew. Through the glass in the front door she caught sight of the couple who had come in earlier. He must have taken flight when he heard their footsteps on the stairs. She stared out. The couple were making their way to the car park. The man was several paces behind the woman and carrying two umbrellas. The sky was slightly lighter than it had been. Sylvie watched for a while. Then she went across to her desk, leant over and pulled the drawer open.

* * *

'Right,' she said in a purposeful voice, not like her own. 'This will sound peculiar because it's hard to translate and it sounds pretty peculiar anyway.' She turned pages over. 'Here it is.'

This would get her nowhere, reading bits to Paul out of books.

'That's the book that got left behind, isn't it? You didn't send it back, then?'

'No.'

She didn't look at him. He waited.

116

'OK. *"Jealousy would have been a relief to her."*'

She stopped. She couldn't leave it at that, but looking at it again it seemed to be the only intelligible sentence.

Paul raised his eyebrows. 'You could have remembered that, couldn't you? Actually, I can't see anything in it. It's not peculiar. What struck you about it?'

'Well, on its own I suppose it isn't that startling. Perhaps it's the part that leads up to it.'

'How does that go, then?'

This was a mistake. 'It sort of goes on a bit, then it says "She fancied once that she detected the agreeable stirring of the brood of jealousy, and found it neither in her heart nor in her mind, but in the book of wishes, well known to the young where they write matter which may sometimes be independent of both those volcanic albums. Jealousy would . . ." etc.' She struggled through it, stopping and starting.

She shut the book but kept hold of it.

'That means something to you, does it?' he said.

'Yes,' she said.

He shook his head. 'I'm glad it helps you. It wouldn't help me.'

'I might go back to London,' she said. 'Do something about George's flat.'

Part Two

CHAPTER ONE

The ceiling was low and unembellished. Sylvie had thrown out the pillows and was lying flat, trying to align the length of her back with the mattress. The central heating was full on; the lights switched off, the window raised. Upstairs a telephone rang and she felt feet crossing the floor. Then, more demandingly, another one rang in the next room. She heard it through the open door. She didn't close her eyes; it was restful looking at the oblique light above her and the broken lines of shadow cast by the cross pieces of the sash window. She slowed down her breathing.

Eventually she picked up her watch from the table beside her and turned it until she could read the face. She thought of lists but she wouldn't make lists. She had done last time, in those days when the days ahead were dark, but not dark enough to conceal all that needed to be done in them. Blackout was what she'd needed. She had written down things she might forget, not the obvious ones like the registry office and the undertaker, but No chrysanthemums, buy black gloves and give money to Justine, how much, question mark. She was George's cleaner. They had looked incongruous and domestic on the page of her note book; nothing to do with her father. She hadn't trusted herself to do anything.

The bed was cool and clean under her. She had made it up with sheets from the cupboard. They still had paper tickets from the laundry pinned to them with stiff safety pins. She hadn't wanted to read them in case they had a date on. But she had done, and discovered that the faint typing at the bottom just said household and the price. She didn't mind lying here half undressed. She had wanted more comfort than the sofa. But it wasn't time to sleep yet, not for hours. She was grateful for that; it allowed her acclimatisation. Rest, not sleeping. People used both words for death as though they were interchangeable. This wasn't stupid; it was truthful. In that place one word was as good as another. No distinctions. No meanings. No chrysanthemums. There weren't any words. There weren't going to be any.

She had known as she walked in earlier that this wasn't a refuge; it wasn't home to anyone. She had put her bags on the hall floor. There was nothing inside to pin her down. She had sensed that, confined as she was by the small unaired rooms behind the closed doors and George's serviceable furniture, she was still in flight. People felt secure in their houses, well balanced even, not realising that it was the familiar objects inside that were propping them up.

The sky was dusky and orange from the street lights. It came into the room. Not like the country where the sky stayed outside. She could still feel the motion of the car. That and the Tunnel, which produced its own sea legs. Too many layers of entombment and everyone pretending the water wasn't on top of them. Fish and sewage and cross Channel ferries and the weight of the water. The occupants of the other cars all carried on reading the paper. Sylvie envied them their distractions and their snail-like ability to make themselves at home. Out came the sandwiches in aluminium foil, the

122

canned drinks and the sports pages. In the curve of a railway tunnel the passengers have a glimpse of what the driver sees; the bored hole and the light approaching. Under the Channel it didn't seem like a tunnel except at the beginning on the downward slope when, if she forgot and looked out, she knew they were sliding into a chute. At the far end, on the upward slope, knowledge returned, but by then her claustrophobia was retrospective, easier to deal with.

The telephone rang again. She left it. It was good to leave things. She knew who it was. It stopped.

She thought, when you go there, however long it takes, between knowing it will happen and getting there, what do you think of? Her mother had taken a long time, Maurice, seconds. Her father, perhaps half an hour. The doctor she had spoken to, at the hospital where he'd been taken, had said shorter, but she hadn't trusted him. He hadn't liked the question. He had been studiedly patient and made eye contact that, though accurate, managed to miss her. He hadn't wanted her to think that they should have done more with the time, used it for rushing through procedures. But that wasn't what she'd meant, not at all. Sylvie thought, sometimes when you can't bear it, something else takes over, a sort of chemical that circulates and holds you still; an antidote to adrenalin. It doesn't numb you, or comfort you, or exempt you. If there's no one there to do that for you, no one who loves you, it takes over.

George had collapsed in the street, not far from home. People in the dry cleaners and the wine bar had both called an ambulance. Only one had turned up, luckily. Sylvie had gone round to

123

thank them.

*   *   *

Sylvie got up and sat on the edge of the bed. She would have to call Paul. He would start to worry where she was. She went into the kitchen without putting her shoes on. The floor was cold under her feet. She dialled the number. It was dinnertime there. She got Felix. He asked her how she was and whether she had had a good journey. He said the restaurant was fairly busy, not bad for a Tuesday. It was freezing, he was only just warming up from his bike ride and the clients were stuffing their faces. He went to fetch Paul. Sylvie waited. There was a muffled thud, then Paul's voice. He said she sounded far away. Felix hadn't said that. He seemed less real than Felix. He said he'd called her twice, where had she been? She said, getting here. Driving into London from Dover, the skyline had changed even in the short time since she'd last done it, more cranes, more incomplete towers to the east of the city. She didn't know why she said it; he wouldn't have been interested. But she could see them now; tall blocks and grilles of scaffolding with the dull light behind. Paul said he hoped she got on well with the estate agent tomorrow; she must be firm about the price. She said thank you and asked if Lucien was all right. He said he was. He had collected him from school and he seemed fine. Natalie had got him to bed. He said she must remember to eat and hoped she would sleep all right. She couldn't wish him the same, not the sleep, it was too early. Here it was even earlier, a whole hour earlier. That made a difference in the evening. Eight and nine felt entirely different. She sent Lucien a kiss and said to tell him she'd speak to him tomorrow. She was sorry when she put the receiver down. It was as if there had been an echo on the line. She wished Paul had picked up the telephone, not Felix; then he would have got the benefit of being the first voice she spoke to, of sounding human.

Paul had mentioned eating. She looked at the blank cupboards, knowing there was food inside them; packet of rice and pasta, jars of pickles, tins of peas and tuna. George hadn't been one for stocking up, because he liked to go out every day, but there would be something. She had seen to the fridge last time. The unopened stuff was no different from what was in the supermarket; things sold for profit and consumption. Dealing with the rest, the pitiful half used things, had been like picking out stones from hard soil with her finger nails. She had kept closing her eyes.

She closed them again now, then re-opened them and put the memory to one side. She told herself what to do, as though she was addressing someone dense. Shut the bedroom window; this was the ground floor. Walk past the mirror. Shoes, coat, bag. Leave lights. Nothing else on. Door keys. Sylvie left George's flat.

* * *

She noticed the dryness of the cold in the street. Going out was like stepping into an unheated room, so her mood didn't alter. She could breathe in the same way as she had done indoors, not needing to take the gasp that registered the shock

125

of damp country air. They had it easy here. She pulled her coat round her and tucked her hair into her collar just the same. It was a habit. The light was pervasive, though it had various sources; bright paned front doors, lighted rooms, street lamps, car lamps, retreating red tail lights. These were insignificant, without poignancy, in the city. Once they disappeared over the hill at home, there was complete darkness. She got to the row of shops, all shut, apart from the late night one and the wine bar. She wasn't paying attention and went in through the shop exit because it was the first door she came to and was then confronted with the man at the till, half hidden behind the pile of Evening Standards and the bucket of colourless carnations in cellophane, last ditch peace offerings. This was where George used to come, when he ran out of basics in between his supermarket trips. He complained about the prices. Sylvie picked up a basket and walked round the wrong way. The man didn't say anything, he wasn't officious, just glanced at her. She couldn't see any obvious science in the arrangement of goods, but was conscious of being back to front and didn't see anything she wanted. Packets of plastic razors, washing powder, disposable nappies, shiny packages of pig-based material welded together, expensive fruit juice, hard looking oranges and a handful of passed over, atrophied vegetables. The shop smelled different from its French equivalent. She started from the beginning again and picked up a packet of coffee and a bottle of Italian wine that would never be allowed in the valley of the Meuse. The bread was tough under its wrappings so it stayed on the shelf. She paid at the till and left.

CHAPTER TWO

When Sylvie got back to the flat she went straight to the kitchen, opened the wine with a type of corkscrew she wasn't used to and took out a glass. They were an odd collection. George must have kept breaking them and replacing them piecemeal. She carried the glass and the bottle into the sitting room and put them on the top of a bookcase. She realised she still had her coat on. She took it off, also her shoes, her rings, her watch and left them in a neat pile on the floor. She poured herself some wine and drank it straight off. She poured more and left the full glass on a bookshelf. She walked over to a cupboard in the corner of the room, bent down and opened its doors, caught the stale pepper smell of stored paper. Sylvie knelt down in front of it. Here was old-fashioned stationery guarding old-fashioned methods of organisation. She didn't want to disturb the arrangements, or be the person about to disturb them. She remembered these things now she saw them: the shoe boxes and buff coloured folders held together with thin brown elastic bands, some single, some put on crossways to stop what was inside from bulging out, the pale grey paper and tissue lined envelopes, yellowing at the corner—untouched since Eve used them. George must have brought them with him to London. Packets of French blotting paper. Newspaper cuttings. Last year's English Christmas stamps held together with a paper clip. Old gas bills, the hot water long run out of the bath. She looked inside without touching, like a child

127

mesmerised by another child's dolls' house. Then she saw what she wanted. A stack of thick white envelopes, loose not bundled together, their tops neatly sliced by a sharp paper knife. She put her hand in and took them out, reconstituted the pile so that what had been at the bottom was on top. Her handwriting hadn't changed much.

In some ways, she felt as if she were reading someone else's letters that she had no business to read. These contained no secrets though: the opposite. Her imagination had nowhere to run to. Anecdotes, observations, snatches of conversation. It was like going on a journey with the landscape filling the inside of the car; nothing on the outside, nothing unknown. She read about twenty of her letters compulsively, one after another, flicking the sheets over, but otherwise not moving. Then she stopped. She sat back on her heels and swallowed, coming up for air. She picked up another batch from the pile and held them on her lap.

She had thought of her life as life size, whatever else it was or it wasn't. These letters showed it reduced and, by this, she didn't mean scaled down. She hadn't produced miniatures, tiny representations on ovals of copper, with a one-haired paintbrush, that satisfied with their completeness. What she'd written about—the restaurant, the clients, Lucien, Paul and his family, Felix, Maude, and what she hadn't necessarily referred to, but was conscious of, the length of the days, the length of the nights, the size of the trees in the forest, the distance between the restaurant and the village, between the village and the town—all of it was less than life size. Petty, dwarfish, as flat as the country she lived in. The proportions, in relation to the number of years,

128

were hardly bearable. There was so much lacking, and, in another way, so much missing. What remained were her own demarcated phrases like tidy hedging.

She remembered, not exactly telling her father everything, she wouldn't have done that, but being expansive, not skimping. She remembered the feeling of writing, as if there were no boundaries between living and disclosing. And George had replied as if he'd known that to be the case. She couldn't understand it. She carried on reading.

After nearly two hours Sylvie got up from the floor. Straightening her legs was uncomfortable; she wasn't used to kneeling. She stood still for a minute and stared at the pile of clothes and jewellery on the floor. She couldn't remember putting them there. They might have been left on a shore, by water, and the owner gone for a swim. She picked up her rings and the watch and slipped them back on. She found her glass of wine, finished it and poured another. She left her letters where they were, in a lopsided heap on the carpet. They didn't belong in the cupboard. She went to the drawer of George's desk and took out some writing paper and an envelope. It was the sort he used, not what she used, but that didn't matter. Jerry Dorney wouldn't care. She had bothered too long about that sort of thing. The right kind of stationery, properly black ink. What did the look of a letter matter? She wrote a short note. She thought of it as homeopathic medicine. A minute dose of the old poison to cure her of the disease.

*   *   *

The following day, Wednesday, she looked for her father's last letter. It might be there somewhere in some state or other; begun, half written, written but not in an envelope, unstamped, ready to post. She searched methodically, almost lazily. She was able to do this because she hadn't lost it. Part of the frenzy of looking was knowing you were responsible. Lost objects represented lost moments. How many more would there be? She went through the flat, opening drawers and cupboards, smoothing the contents if she disarranged them. George's clothes were carefully folded, smelling old and wholesome. He kept the odds and ends—shoe laces, sticking plaster, out of date ear drops—with the light bulbs in a box in the kitchen. She left everything as she found it. It was a kind of faithfulness. That's how she saw it. The flat was quiet, with a daytime quiet. She felt calm, like a child safely occupied and the morning stretching ahead. In the end she wasn't looking for anything. It was more like slow spring cleaning without the bucket of soapy water.

Paul called in the afternoon and put Lucien on. He answered yes and no to Sylvie's questions and left gaps when he smiled in reply and expected her to see. She carried on, until he told her a complete story about Bernard swapping his watch for two batteries that didn't work. He and Bernard knew they didn't work because they tested them. She said it sounded clever and rather complicated. They blew each other kisses. Paul came back on the line. He wanted to know how she had got on with instructing an estate agent and she told him she hadn't done that yet. He asked her what she had been doing, then, and she'd said sorting stuff out, going through George's things. He was silent for a few seconds, then he said he hoped that wasn't too painful. Sylvie was conscious of misleading him. He would see her emptying cupboards, gathering stuff into bags for the charity shop, putting essential documents into files. Had he known what she was really doing, he would have been puzzled. Her resentment at this potential reaction got into her voice when she replied. She said it wasn't painful, as long as she knew she could take her time over it, if she had to hurry it would be. He said he wasn't hassling her, he wished he could help, that was all. He loved her. Then she felt sorry and guilty, and, before she thought, she found herself saying that she was worried that one of George's papers was missing. He said she should ask the solicitor and she said it wasn't like that. He asked what it was and she said she wasn't sure, so he said, if she didn't know what it was, how could she know it was missing. She said she sensed something had gone. He said, sarcastic, perhaps she should inform the police. She said they wouldn't be able to help. He said, let's go back a bit, was this thing official or personal? She couldn't say personal, he'd be on to it, so she said she really didn't know. Who does know, he asked. Sylvie said she supposed George did. He said you'd better try a fucking medium then. She didn't reply to that, so he took a deep breath in an exasperated way, and said, look, he was sorry, it was hard talking to her on the telephone, it made him feel useless. And she said, that was all right, she didn't mean to make him feel like that. And he said he wasn't blaming her, then they said goodbye. She hadn't finished talking to Lucien, but she couldn't ask for him back after all

131

that. She hoped he'd already run away and wasn't hanging around listening.

*   *   *

The next day, Thursday, she heard from Jerry at about the time that she gave up expecting to. They arranged to meet in a bar near his office.

At five o'clock she had a bath, got dressed, travelled east to meet him. It was a fixed point to look forward to. It had been her second complete day in George's flat and she hadn't done anything useful.

CHAPTER THREE

There were strangers here keeping boredom at bay. They were making an effort; to shriek, to laugh, to ignore the time, to loosen their ties, to hitch up their skirts, to eat without thinking, to keep drinking. This was an interlude. There might be one again tomorrow, but who could tell? Work was as far away as death.

One man was pulled back, caught by his mobile. He cupped a hand to his free ear, walked away from the crowd, bent as if in abdominal pain, talked figures.

They weren't all too young for her, or too raucous—but she thought of Jerry. Alone in this crowd she thought of him, even though she hardly knew him. The half step she'd taken from not knowing him at all had carried her here. She was anxious about the moment of meeting. The music was loud. She had drunk a quarter of the bottle quickly and was now watching the level.

No one was dancing but they kept moving in their seats, shifting from elbow to elbow, tipping their chairs, crossing and re-crossing their legs, clasping their ankles, making abrupt English gestures that stopped short of contact. She watched them but kept an eye on the entrance; revolving doors that were out of keeping with the bare brick and concrete. Jerry walked in. He must have seen her through the radiating panels of glass because he walked straight over to her. She was surprised he recognised her. She wasn't distinctive.

'I'm sorry I'm late,' he said.

He had suggested they meet up in a bar on the old West India Docks, in the shadow of the Canary Wharf towers. They'd agreed on the time. He must have known he wasn't late. He said it because she'd got there first and it was an easy greeting.

'You're not. I was early,' she said. 'I walked about for a bit, but it was getting cold so I came in. I've already started on the wine.'

'I'll catch up.'

He sat down, facing her and the sheer wall of window behind her.

'Have some,' Sylvie said. 'The clean one is yours. I was going to say empty, then I realised mine was too.'

She poured a glass for him. She hoped he hadn't counted on going over to the bar, waiting there, finding change, walking back.

'You've come from upstairs somewhere?' she said.

'More or less. Along and up, yes.'

'It doesn't seem like London,' she said.

The windows looked on to water. He glanced out through the reflection of his face and the back of her head. She was conscious of her neat French haircut, as if Jean-Guy were holding up the mirror to show her his handiwork. She never knew what to say when he did that. It was seven o'clock and had been dark since half past four. She thought of the view behind her. She had looked at it before she sat down. It didn't seem English, but she hadn't been able to place it. Dutch perhaps, or Scandinavian. The buildings, lit up on the far side, rose in steps. The river was too wide for comfortable London bridges. Cleaned up and tamed, railed in for safety, it stretched out and shimmered blackly.

'It's very strange,' Jerry said, 'the way people lean on the guard rail, over there, with their backs to the river. They talk and look up at the buildings. It's natural to stare at water. But they don't seem to want to.'

'Perhaps they're afraid of drowning,' said Sylvie.

'You couldn't drown here. They wouldn't let you.'

'Why not? What else won't they let you do?'

'You can't jump in front of a train. Or down the gap. They've got those sliding doors at the edge of the platform to seal off the drop.'

'I noticed. They're like empty shop windows. I found it confusing.'

'The Jubilee Line Extension,' he said. He paused, as if he were beginning a poem but only knew the title, then he said, 'I've never even been down there. It takes a lot to get me on to public transport. People say they admire the architecture of the new stations. As something to say, it probably has about another year in it.'

'So how do you get here?'

'I slog it out in the traffic. Staring into the sun, if there is any, morning and evening. Through Tower Hamlets.'

'You don't like it here, do you?'

'Not particularly.'

'Does anyone?'

'They complain, but they've got used to it, they seem at home.'

'Which bit of home?'

He thought.

'A bedroom. There are blinds to cut down glare—and pin point lighting. Everyone drinking glasses of water, going to fill them up from a sort of udder, then tucking themselves back in with their computer terminals.'

'You make them sound docile.'

'No. I've given you the wrong idea. They're peevish, full of wants. One day I'll come in and find them under blankets, wearing ear plugs and eye shades expecting to be transported across the Atlantic.'

'What age are they?'

'Young. Really young. They make me feel old and deaf.'

Sylvie poured what remained in the wine bottle into their glasses. Because she owned a restaurant she was used to doing it unassumingly. She suddenly felt lighter, frivolous even. She was relieved Jerry was real, nothing to do with her. Something had happened to him lodged in her imagination; although incorporeal, he hadn't floated free. She felt glad for both of them that they didn't know each other. The note she had sent him had been casual. She had simply mentioned that she was in London.

*   *   *

'I might take up smoking again. Get out of the nursery and join the adolescents on the fire escapes,' he said.

'I saw them,' she said.

She had caught sight of them when she'd walked between the high buildings. They had looked precarious. Exposed in their dark suits, with the wind whipping round the block.

'I had a cigarette the other day. I hadn't had one for about twenty years,' she said.

'What made you?' It was the first question he'd asked her. She had been asking too many.

'I was in a bar and someone gave me one.'

She thought of Jacques. His way of stubbing out a cigarette, as though, if he didn't persecute it, it would re-ignite. She wondered what he would make of it here; the crowds and expanses of floor.

'My wife would find out,' Jerry said. 'That's the drawback. She takes any carelessness with my health as a personal reproach.'

'She looks after you,' Sylvie said.

'I often think it would be a relief to her if I predeceased her. Flagrantly.'

'Is there an ideal length of time, do you think, for being a widow?'

'You tell me,' he said.

'It's probably one of those things you can't tell in advance,' she said. 'Does she work here too?'

He looked puzzled.

'Your wife?'

'Gillian? No, she's miles away. She hardly ever comes to London.'

He looked past Sylvie and out at the water. She was glad he didn't launch into questions he didn't need to know the answer to. Are you in London long? Where did you learn such good English? She imagined a queue of different sized people at Tower Bridge and one of those open-top tourist buses. He didn't ask the questions. It was as restful as being alone. Both their glasses were empty.

'I'll go and get some more, shall I?' he said.

She didn't shake her head, so he got up and went to the bar. She wondered if her letter was in his pocket. From her, a strange woman, meaning strange, not a stranger. He might have read it,

137

finishing a cup of coffee, and left it on the kitchen table. Then, on his way out he'd have picked it up and slipped it in his jacket. There was nothing really in the letter. Nothing anyone would find interesting.

The girl who was serving him left him to answer the telephone. The boy further along the bar stood idle. Jerry didn't bother him. He waited for the girl to finish her conversation. He came back to their table, poured wine for them both. Sylvie took a sip. It was different from what she had chosen, without being nicer.

'You don't want a place up a mountain, do you?' he said. 'I have a house in the Vosges, but we never go there. I'm going to have to sell it.'

'I'm supposed to be selling my father's flat,' Sylvie said. 'That's why I'm here, but I haven't got on with it. I haven't done anything much.' She was aware of her fingertips tense on the base of her glass. 'I started reading the letters I wrote to him. It was a mistake.'

'That sort of thing is. I don't know why it should be, but it is,' he said.

He leant back in his chair, stretched out his legs. She relaxed too and adjusted her feet. He hadn't noticed the change in her tone of voice.

'When the office moved over here,' he said. 'I threw a lot of papers out. My secretary said I should do it. She rigged up a black bin liner, sellotaped it to the edge of my desk. Norma has something of the Girl Guide about her. I'd forgotten about the personal stuff. It quite cheered me up to find it. I thought reading old letters might be a laugh. I should have just chucked them.'

'They were embarrassing?'

138

'Worse.'

'But you knew what was in them?'

'I honestly couldn't remember most of it.'

'So what did you expect?'

'A slice of life. Mine, but a bit removed.'

'It wasn't?'

'I mean some of it must have been a nice surprise at the time, but I couldn't get any sense of that back. Absolutely no sense of nice surprise at the time,' he said.

'So?' she said.

'There was one, a circle with spikes coming out of it and words in boxes, like something from the report and accounts. I thought, when I opened it, she was giving me advice about strategy. Bloody patronising, but I was big enough to overlook that. Then I looked at it properly and discovered she was writing about our relationship. Flow charts, that's what they're called. Not a love letter. None of them were love letters.'

'I'm sorry,' Sylvie said.

'I'm not saying I behaved well, or that I didn't deserve these travesties. Polemics about where we stood and where we were going, laced with darlings and available dates. I couldn't decide whether there was something truly wrong with me or it was a sign of the times.'

'At least you hadn't written them.'

'Somehow that didn't make any difference.'

'Who was she?'

'Oh, a former work colleague,' he said.

He fell quiet and Sylvie thought, he's either forgotten or he doesn't want to remember any more.

'I liked the book you left behind. You should

139

have read it,' she said.

He shook his head. He wasn't interested. She wondered whether to ask him about the daughter who had given it to him, or to think of something else. He had suddenly sunk. He had allowed himself to, as if he knew her very well, or she wasn't there at all. What did you say to men when that happened to them? Where was their resilience? She looked at him and the expression on his face and thought, it's a reflection of their physiognomy, they go soft and feel terrible. It's all to do with beefing them up again. Could she be bothered? What she didn't say, at this point, was, what's the matter? She had learned that much.

'I tried reading a bit of the book to my husband. It was a mistake. He didn't get it, but he never would have done. It wasn't just my feeble translation. He resists because it's written in English. He finds it threatening.'

He was still silent and she remembered how he had looked, sitting alone at the restaurant table. She remembered his silence. It was his talking that surprised her.

'What did you do with your letters?' she said.

He bucked up a bit. 'I shredded them.'

He looked at her again, then away, out at the darkness behind, as though he were following their committal.

*   *   *

The revolving door kept turning, flinging out more and more people. They came out clumsily, missing the rhythm of it. Overcoats, suits, briefcases, heavy umbrellas, telephones; nothing that distinguished their gender. Sylvie couldn't help staring at them. She had a sense that she was facing all this life and Jerry was missing it.

'You said when you called you had a dinner to go to,' she said.

It wasn't that she wanted to lose him, she didn't. But he had to leave anyway. She might as well look after him.

'Tonight?'

'I think that's what you said.'

He pulled a printed sheet of paper from his pocket, not even a diary.

'Christ, you're right,' he said, 'How did you know? Will you be all right? Can I get a cab for you?'

'I'll be fine.'

He picked up his glass and took two gulps. He put his hands on the table and half got up. He looked across at Sylvie and got stuck, puzzled that she hadn't mirrored him.

'I'll stay,' she said. 'I'm not in a hurry.'

He stood up straight. She remained where she was. He looked worried, torn between being a confident English schoolboy or a recessive one.

'I've enjoyed this evening,' she said.

'Let's meet again before you go back.'

'I'd like that,' she said.

*   *   *

She went back on the Underground. She basked in the harsh lighting and studied the other passengers' faces. She felt she was seeing everything clearly. She got out at her station and walked up the wooden slatted escalator. Compared with where she had just come from in Docklands, it felt like a branch line of a country railway. Outside it was beginning to be frosty. She appreciated the rush of cold on her face, the exhilaration of breathing, the empty echoes of her shoes on the pavement. She liked having a key in her pocket. At the restaurant she rarely used one. She got it out too early, four street lamps too early. By the time she reached George's flat it had turned from hot to cold in her fingers.

CHAPTER FOUR

Without Paul lying next to her, Sylvie could indulge her insomnia. She had slept for about an hour and woken, in the way of a cork pulled out of a bottle. The dream she'd been dreaming had been mean, not voluminous. It had squeezed her out. She couldn't recall it and she couldn't have stayed there. She got up and wrapped her jersey round her shoulders, walked into the kitchen. There was enough light to see by. The dark wasn't solid. She filled the kettle with water, banged it down on the stove, lit the jet. Blue flames shot with orange, as compelling as a camp fire for staring at, at this time of night. The gas blew into the silence.

'Go back to bed, darling,' Eve used to say as Sylvie stood in the doorway. 'We're not getting out again once we're in. And I shall turn the light off in a minute and that will be that. Quick, quick.' Mostly Sylvie ran back to her bedroom, swindled by magic thinking, not because she was afraid of the dark. That will be that. What was 'that'? Once or twice she defied the instruction, she was that sort of child, and then she saw it happen. Her father, whose back was towards her, manoeuvring himself from a sitting to a lying position, displacing swathes of sheet, her mother leaving her side of the bed linen taut, slithering in. They snuggled under, only Eve's left arm perpendicular, shapely, reaching for the lamp switch. 'Sylvie, I meant it.' Then darkness. The wonder of it, the trust of these grown people in giving themselves up to sleep, to the helplessness of it. She could hardly have been more astonished

143

had they agreed to fall backwards from standing. Sometimes she would wake and hear them talking. The subdued up and down notes of night time conversation. She envied them the companionship. She didn't know about lovemaking, but, if the outward forms had been boiled down, she would have understood the essence of it. She would have envied them that too.

Sylvie took her tea to bed with her. She half sat up, her knees bent, both hands warm round the mug. She let her mind drift. She didn't use the time for thinking. It was an abuse of thought to cram it into surplus hours of sleeplessness. She knew the process; the apparently provisional opening, falsely provisional, as there was no going back on it, the agitation that worked up to a crisis without resolution, the compulsion to begin again, having failed to reach it. Each sequence got shorter and more panicky. Nothing in the daytime corresponded to it. No, that wasn't true. Looking for things could be like that.

It was peaceful in the bedroom. Sylvie liked being alone and she liked the still shapes round her. The walls seemed notional; flimsy partitions between city dwellers, as vague as the half light. She didn't feel separate. She put her empty mug on the floor by the bed and got under the covers.

*　　　*　　　*

The next morning Sylvie blew the dust off the telephone directories and sat, before she got dressed, with the Yellow Pages on her bare knees. There was nothing between spin dryers and sports clubs. She wasn't surprised. She sipped her coffee and bit into one of George's digestive biscuits. What she was after had no substance. She was also relieved. The remains of Eve's upbringing made her wary of taking on anyone who hadn't been personally recommended. It was a practical problem, though, in other ways, spectral. She intended to be brisk about it. She waited until nine thirty, by which time she presumed he would have finished his breakfast, and then called Graham.

He pretended to remember her, having asked her to remind him of her connection with St John the Evangelist. She spoke of George's funeral and Don, and said she hoped his Appeal was going well. He explained some of the successes so far, without being touched that she had bothered to mention it. She pressed on and said she would like help from a dependable spiritualist. Did he know of one in his Parish? She trusted his judgement. He spluttered a bit. Then said Ah, she was French, wasn't she, and although spiritual guidance wasn't really his forte, he would do his best for her. Bereavement was often a difficult time. She could pop round for ten minutes before the woman from English Heritage appeared. He hoped financial assistance would be forthcoming from that quarter. No, Sylvie said, she had meant spiritualist, a medium. She needed to consult one. He said he certainly knew of no such person and was alarmed that she should think he would do. Disappointed women who preyed on other disappointed women and told them what they wanted to hear. Not of course, that the male of the species, of whom he was one, was exonerated; they were, more often than not, the cause of the disappointment. She said she hadn't meant to offend him, she would ask at the dry cleaners. He paused, then he said he believed there was somewhere in Belgravia, The Spiritualist Society of Great Britain or some such. She said, so there is such a place, she knew they would be regulated. He said she must see it in the same way that she would see the regulation of quick-fix exhaust mechanics, laughed twice, and asked if she believed in Purgatory. Certainly not, she said. What came next would either be nothing or glorious. Rather the former, he said he assumed, but he'd asked because he thought that that particular doctrine, if you could call it that, had led to tinkering in the hinterland. That sounds like a Christmas pantomime, she said. Will you be here, he asked, we're always short of contraltos and Hesther who ran the choir might come up with a French carol. Sylvie thanked him nicely and retreated. They said goodbye to each other cordially, each pleased to have managed to get on with another person so different. Why had he thought she was contralto?

*   *   *

Joyce sat straight up on a piano stool and her eyes fixed on the space between them.

'There are a lot of them coming, Sylvie. Might be a choir. Or a school. I think they're all boys, men. Do you have a family photo with a lot of men in?'

She glanced encouragingly at Sylvie and then re-focused on the space. It was as though she had two sets of eyes. Their ways of looking were so different. Her voice stayed the same in both modes: chatty.

146

'Maybe.'

'That's how I'm seeing it. Like a whole group of them clustering round. They're all happy to come. Some of them wearing waistcoats. Edmund, I think it's Edmund, he's coming forward. He's smiling and nodding. He's patting something. Could it be your head, Sylvie? He says he's very fond of you, keeping an eye. He's concerned about your eating. Your eating habits getting into winter; carbohydrates, he mentions, and bigger portions. Don't let the dinner get cold, he says, or you won't find it appetising. I wonder why he thinks you might do that? Salad. He's shaking his head about salad. Yes, definitely plates of food. Can you take that?'

'Sorry?'

'Does food mean something in your life?'

'Yes, I suppose it does.'

'He says he's looking out for you. Here's another one. This one's got a beard. He's walking slowly along a path. He keeps stopping to lean over. Flowers, it could be, by the path. He looks happy, he says he's happy around flowers. Do you have anyone, Sylvie, fond of gardening?'

'I don't think so. No.'

'He sees your gifts. I wondered if it might be your father or grandfather. An older man in your life. He thought they might be in horticulture, your gifts. He loves the summer. He says you love the summer too. He says next summer will be your time. It will all come together for you. There will be great benefits to your family when this happens. He feels you're upset about a dear one in your family. They're all men, dear, keep coming, I don't know whether you're content with that. They keep smiling and stepping forward. This one's holding something. I think it's a glass. He's raising it to you. Did your father like a drink, Sylvie? He's saying it gets him by. Could that be him? His eyes are like yours, sad like yours, but he wants you to know he isn't sad where he is now. Just keep that. He's a cultivated man, your father. Pictures is it, or antiques? He's somewhere with pictures and he's showing one to a child. An Impressionist, I'd say it was. I think the little child could be one of yours. He's very attached to it. Very proud. I'm sure it's a grandchild. They're both looking at the scene and he's pointing at an animal in it. A cat or a dog. I wonder if one of your children likes pets? Or it could be your father likes pets.'

Sylvie thought, I'm listening to this because my husband said go and see a fucking medium then, without for a moment believing I would do.

The room was insipidly decorated and over heated, sealed against draughts and outside noises. For a woman's house it seemed impersonal; blank, not minimalist. There were two basketwork chairs and a television. The Aeolian chimes over the window and the beaded curtain that hid the kitchen were the only blandishments and no air currents stirred them. There was nothing else to coax the spirits and, although Joyce was on the piano stool, no piano. Sylvie glanced over her shoulder to see if it was behind her, but it wasn't.

Joyce's voice stopped.

'Sorry?' Sylvie said.

'Just give me your father's name, if you would.'

'George de Mora.'

'George,' said Joyce.

In the silence, Sylvie chose not to look at her.

She remembered now why she had come here. It was nothing to do with Paul. The hassle of calling the Spiritualist society, getting hold of Joyce, finding her way on two buses, turning the A to Z upside down, to work out which way to go, in the pattern of small streets. It hadn't been spitefulness.

'Is there anything you'd like to ask George since he's with us, Sylvie?'

'You could ask him if he replied to my last letter.' She sounded serious and heard it in her own voice. She saw the change in Joyce's eyes, a more personal interest, but, when the woman started speaking again, she knew she'd get more of the same.

'He's surrounded by books; quite a few shelves of them. He has a great love of books. I would say that they're lining the walls. Am I right in thinking he was a librarian in his working days? No? I feel that's what he would have wished, to work in a library. I just want to give you that. He's smiling, dear, but he's being very selective. I don't think he's going to answer that question.'

'Fine,' said Sylvie.

She knew, as she half listened to Joyce, what had been missing from her letters to her father. The sleep and sleeplessness, the daydreams, absences of mind, gaps between thoughts, hourly annihilations. Were these some sort of preparation for what lasted so long? George had doggedly read what she'd written and written back, as if her life had substance. He'd sent it back thicker.

'I'm looking to see who else is there. I can't at present locate any women, but we can hope for your mother. She has passed hasn't she? She's here somewhere.'

149

'Please don't go to any more trouble.'

'It isn't a trouble, Sylvie. Was she a good looker?'

'It must be tiring though,' said Sylvie. 'Yes, everyone thought she was beautiful. We could have a cup of tea.'

'They're all at their best, dear. In their prime, one and all.'

Sylvie wanted to go, but she felt uneasy about leaving too quickly, shutting the front door with George and the unknown relations still inside the house. At the end of Joyce's working day, did they slip back; held in place by glass and a finite edge? Or were they shifting about, concerned for those they had left behind? All that advice and interference and love, unspent, kept in check.

'It's up to you, Sylvie. I've set aside the time. We can always resume.' Joyce leant back and fumbled behind the piano stool. 'I'll just switch off the cassette player. People like a tape to take home with them.'

The steady hum that Sylvie had assumed was the overstretched heating system stopped.

CHAPTER FIVE

'She was different away from the spirits. I enjoyed talking to her. She had been an elocution teacher and an artist's model.'

'That's a quiet profession,' said Jerry.

They were back at the same table as the evening before. He looked at Sylvie, not beyond her at the water. They were both glad to see each other.

'She seemed infected by their company. Like a child who picks up tricks of speech or bad language. She reproduced their banality. But why should they be banal?'

'It's the condition. You can tell because it seeps into extreme old age. Like intimations of immortality only the other end on. My mother and her sister, Lou, have conversations of numbing deadliness. How many were there, says Aunt Lou, A good many, says Ma. Lou's asking about church and Ma hasn't even been there. They can carry on for hours.'

'They're both senile?'

'My mother isn't, but she gets into the swing of it and you can't tell the difference between them.'

'Do they live with you?'

'Christ, no. Though sometimes it feels like it. They're a presence.

*   *   *

'It's quieter here tonight,' she said.

'Friday. People go away, or home, or somewhere. Thursday's their night out.'

151

'You don't?'

'Home? Yes. I sit in traffic with everyone else.'

He wasn't though. He was here.

'I ought to go back. But I haven't done anything. None of the things I was supposed to do,' she said.

'You've seen me and a medium.'

'They weren't scheduled.'

'And read your own letters.'

'All but one, yes.'

'Which was that?'

She could see it, at the bottom of the pile, folded identically.

'The last one. I didn't get a reply to it.'

'That's what you asked Joyce about?'

There was no logic to what she'd just told him. Not re-reading a letter because it hadn't got a response. He didn't point it out.

She said, 'I wrote to my father and said I was leaving Paul and coming to London. Leaving for good, I mean.'

She would be able to remember what she'd written, if she let herself. But it wasn't immediately to hand. One of those memories like a thin, deep pit, which it is possible to skirt around. She knew Jerry wasn't going to be curious in the wrong sort of way. She continued.

'I wasn't asking him anything. But once I'd written it, I got stuck. I waited. It hung there, this idea, without becoming anything. George didn't call me and he didn't reply, though I think he had time to. I told him I wouldn't actually leave until I heard from him. I don't know why I said that.'

He looked at her. 'Then you couldn't leave.'

'Not then,' she said.

It hadn't been a confession or a complaint, so he

didn't commiserate. Neither did he offer advice. She felt as if she was relating a story of everyday life. Like one of Joyce's narrations, it seemed not to be attached to anything.

*   *   *

'How old is your son, did you say?'

'Five,' she said.

'Do you want to order something to eat?' he said. 'We can't just carry on drinking all evening. Well, we could do. You seem to be up for it, though I remember reading somewhere that French women aren't.'

'I'm half English. I'm not George's daughter for nothing. But let's eat.'

*   *   *

'How do they manage without you? At the restaurant.'

'Maude comes in. She was there that evening you were, because of the party. She's rather striking. Vivacious.'

'I don't think I remember her.'

'No?'

'No.'

'My husband likes her.'

'And?'

'I don't know. Yes, I suppose I do.'

*   *   *

'The man died, didn't he?'

Sylvie nodded. She noticed she didn't mind his

153

asking. She didn't recoil inside as she had done when anyone else had mentioned it.

'They made enough noise afterwards,' he said. 'It was still pissing with rain but they wound down their windows and carried on talking and beeping and yelling goodnight to each other.'

'I thought you said you slept through it?'

'Did I? When did I say that?'

'I asked you the next morning and you said you hadn't heard anything.'

'I can't remember saying that, but that doesn't mean anything. Did you look worried?'

'Possibly.'

'I wouldn't have wanted you to be worried.'

*   *   *

'I had to send flowers,' Sylvie said. 'Everyone said I should. It seemed a bit sick really.'

'Do you always do what everyone wants?'

'No.' She paused. 'It might look as if I do. It doesn't feel like that. My husband thought it might occur to me to send the ones that Maurice's wife left behind in the general chaos. They were her share of the retirement present. That shows how unaccommodating he thinks I am. Perverse, anyway. Maude went to the funeral. She called in on the way back and told us about it. She was carrying a missal. It looked rather well thumbed. I think it must have been her grandmother's. It had the order of service tucked in it. She got it out to show Paul. They had this pious conversation about the numbers of celebrants and mourners, and the glossiness of the coffin. They talk like that about the menu plans. Serious.'

'Sanctimonious.'

They finished their supper without hurrying. There were only a few people left and they were all at far away tables; no one at the bar, just the disconsolate pair behind it who had been there the evening before. There were fewer lights on in the nearby buildings, so the water was blacker, shimmering patchily. Sylvie knew she could choose between taking Jerry and leaving him. It wasn't indifference. She had a clear sense of his assurance and vulnerability, the precise amounts and mixture of which are crucial to sexual attraction. She also knew that this knowledge came as much from her as from him and was not transferable. Another woman would arrive at a different calibration. The clear sightedness felt dangerous, more like the strange wellbeing that precedes illness than matter-of-fact health. The music was loud, but it didn't bind anyone together. It was an extra, insular presence. Sylvie and Jerry got up, walked across to the bar to pay. He didn't touch her, but they stood near each other, almost touching, aware of the exact distance between them. They had to wait while the girl put stoppers in bottles and pumped the air out.

*   *   *

He said he would take her home. They went in his car and he probably shouldn't have been driving. They set off from an underground car park. The streets they passed through were unimportant and the moon was caught on the edge of the roofs. It was a bit of reality, something to look at. He knew where he was going, until the last half mile, then he needed Sylvie's help. He asked her for help and she told him where to turn off the main road. Then she had to keep telling him. She told him where to stop. There was the door to George's flat, the window to the left, the curtains left open so she could make out the forms of the furniture inside, the mirror over the mantelpiece catching the street light, and the silhouette of the dark jug with the round handle deflecting it. Incongruous to see it. The stopping was final. She felt lost—missing telling him what to do and his doing it. He leaned over and kissed her. She shifted until they fitted into the space available, as if it were a third party they were kind enough to accommodate. They could have stayed in the car, but this was a residential street in a genteel part of London.

Their contact was broken by moving from the comfortable darkness, into the lighted hall, and by standing up and walking. Jerry followed her into her father's flat and it was less disconcerting than it might have been. She thought for a second, when she turned to him and his face was close, but not so close that she could no longer see him, he's going to make excuses. The momentary dismay in his eyes, and the way his fingers flexed against her back made her think, suddenly, he's going to say he has sexual difficulties. She thought, do men ever admit to it, and why would he have come back with me? All at the same moment, he pulled her closer against him. She knew that the resistance had come from her and transferred to him and that he'd overcome it. And, having been nearly disappointed, even though it had been fleeting and imaginary and quickly reversed, she felt relief undo her, and she could be undone, because it had only been a

156

moment, not half a lifetime. He would have felt her relief, without knowing the cause. He wouldn't have mistaken it for passion, though the feeling was the same, and the letting go.

*   *   *

'What are you doing today, then?' he asked her, once they'd woken up thoroughly. They lay side by side, touching, conscious of the daylight, but not bothered by it. Sylvie had slept peacefully in George's bed. She assumed Jerry had too. He hadn't disturbed her.

'I'll drive back this afternoon or tomorrow. I haven't decided. Probably today. They'll get worried, start checking up on me. Not that sort of checking up. Paul bothers about my state of mind, not my faithfulness.'

'I can't see much wrong with your state of mind. I ought to try to be home for lunch,' Jerry said.

They stayed prosaic until they parted. They didn't mind what they said to each other but neither of them needed to say anything memorable.

CHAPTER SIX

It was late when Sylvie got back to the restaurant on Saturday evening. She walked in to the smell of the end of dinner. She felt slightly sickened by it but didn't trust her judgement. It might have been real or merely a sensory association with the sight of used plates and dishes. There was no opportunity for a controlled experiment, the beginning and end never happened at once. Then there was the coffee, dark and tarnished. That gave away chronology. She might have been feeling sick anyway. The motorway traffic had moved in waves, through grey mist. She took a few steps into the dining room, carrying her car keys and conscious of wearing the ordinary clothes she'd travelled in. She recognised, from the tables, the slight dishevelment of later evening; clouded wine glasses, scrunched up napkins, random pieces of unused cutlery, spectacle cases. And in the clients, the slackening of posture and of facial muscles, the moisture at the hairline from heat and mild exertion. The nearest they get to post coital, she thought; they stop chewing. A man with an empty brandy glass, and a woman with a dog asleep on her feet, both stared at her. After a few seconds the woman nodded at her, realising who she was. The man caught his wife's gesture out of the corner of his eye and imitated her. His face stayed aloof. They were regulars. Maude was standing by the corner table where Jerry had sat. She nodded and tipped her head to one side as she talked. She had a perfect row of buttons down the back of her dress,

158

at least one of which would have been impossible for her to do up herself. Sylvie smiled at the couple with the dog, then walked out again.

She didn't meet anyone in the hall. The guests were all in the dining room. The wood-burning stove was alight, safe behind its thick glass doors. Sylvie could smell it now. She went along the downstairs corridor and turned the odd double corner that separated them from the rest of the building. Their flat felt warm, as she went in, and someone had left lights on. Lucien's door was shut. Natalie always closed it once he'd fallen asleep. Sylvie sensed him there in his dark room, but she didn't go in. Sometimes she could look at him without waking him, but at others, he seemed, in his unconsciousness, to be expecting her. Then he would sit straight up and want to know exactly which bit of the evening they'd got to. He would know Paul was in the kitchen, but she wasn't as conveniently confined. She ended up sitting on the bed and mapping her movements for him. If she rushed, it all took longer. Then she had to promise to come back in half an hour.

She went into their bedroom and switched off the lamp. The window was cut off from the winter, by the curtains, lined and interlined and pelmetted. Sylvie went across and opened them. The leaves had gone. And where, before she had left for England, the view had been baffled by them, now it was visible through bare branches, broken by their patterns, but plainer for that. Beyond the first line of trees, she could see the farm track, marked by wooden posts and amateurish loops of telephone wires, and the water-filled furrow at the corner of the field, where the tractor turned. Further on, beyond the second line of trees, the sky was concentrated in the spaces between the branches, a colour between black and the weak sulphurous yellow that came off the village lamps, made of both equally and therefore without a name. The disappearance of the leaves was a surprise, but Sylvie remembered that she had had the surprise before. It happened every year, in the last week of November or the first one of December.

Her hands were damp from the window sill. She rubbed them dry on her jeans. She was sustained by the view, though troubled that it went with the windows on this side of the hotel, as surely as if it had been painted on behind them, changing with the weather and seasons and time of day or night, in a way that indicated a tricksy artist, rather than a life of their own. She liked the dull reflections in the water and imagined herself setting off into them without shoes, to glide or sink. She was kept afloat by Jerry. She felt him still with her, physically present. Amazing how long you could make it last. Though not for ever, obviously. If their desire for each other had been wine in two glasses, not bacchanalian in quantity, she had found that the amount didn't matter. Because the levels matched and there had been no falseness, the glasses had miraculously filled to the brim. She could see him, as he was, a man in middle age; without the gloss of having seen him in his youth and allowing that to add shine. She thought of him in the house in the Thames valley. She saw him walking about in a room, one hand in a back pocket. She saw the fireplace and the rug in front of it and the sofa and chairs and the view from that window across the garden. It was all explicit and recognisable, though

160

she knew it would disappear, if she tried to express the detail in words to herself, just as the look of dreams disappeared once she was out of them. She was thankful for having the picture at all, realising that not knowing meant at least as much as knowing, to her, and that the not knowing part was real, without being factually accurate. He hadn't said anything about seeing her again.

Sylvie heard a car coming up the road towards the restaurant taking the slight incline at speed. Whoever was driving made a noisy extempore stop as though he had met a deer or was pretending to be young. Maude's husband got out and leant with one arm on the polished roof. He couldn't see Sylvie at the unlit window. The kids usually sat in the back, three of them, all strapped in, but the back was dark and empty. She waited. Maude walked over the gravel, her head uncovered, smart shoes moving briskly, an air of being insulated from the cold by her own body heat. She opened the opposite door, sat down in the passenger seat, her legs tastefully arranged and her feet resting on the ground. Her husband stayed where he was and began to talk to someone over the top of the car. It was Paul he was talking to. Their breath condensed in the air. Maude smiled up. The roof overlay her, keeping her safe and in place, and Alain, her husband, was in charge of the roof. Paul glanced down at Maude, but ignored her. Her head was level with his slightly curving stomach, not that far from it, and their feet nearly touching.

Sylvie wasn't part of the spectacle, though she wondered whether she might not have caused it. She had gone away again. Perhaps there had been some irregularity in Maude's timekeeping or behaviour. As far as she could remember Alain had never escorted Maude home from the restaurant before. The dialogue between the two men continued, the words didn't matter. She couldn't hear them anyway through the glass. She saw their speech, as if it were scattered on a page. Chopped up bits of the local newspaper, or the football results; nothing controversial. Their shoulders talked. Neither could see each other below chest level. Sylvie put her hands in the opposite sleeves of her jacket for comfort and warmth, as if she were actually there outside in the cold. The walls gave her no protection. She could use being inside as an excuse, but it wasn't one. She looked away and wished it was daytime and summer. It was easier to be a spare part in the heat. You could settle yourself on the steps or a wall, close your eyes; just you and the sun.

*　　　*　　　*

She didn't see Paul until he came to their room to get ready for bed. He must have known she was back. He would have seen her car. He pretended he hadn't noticed and that he was surprised to see her. This must have been the decision he had come to and she understood that it was easier for both of them. When she saw the made up surprise in his eyes she went and kissed him so that she shouldn't see it any longer and because she was grateful to him for sparing her. He felt solid and familiar against her and the dishonesty was part of the feeling. He slackened his hold, without quite letting her go, and asked her how she'd got on in London and what the weather had been like and if there had been much traffic on the motorway. None of the questions was difficult to answer. She thought, this is how people talk to each other most of the time and she relaxed into it, as if it were a pillow full of inexhaustible feathers, that you could choose not to feel as interminable. Paul moved away from her and sat on the edge of the bed to undo his shoes.

'I've been looking at dates.' He disengaged the laces logically, no tugging.

'And?' She said this encouragingly, not aggressively.

He didn't look up. 'Can you remember what we did last time Christmas was on a Monday?'

'Was Eve still alive?' said Sylvie.

'I don't know. I'd have to work it out. Five years ago was it, with lcap years, something like that? Was she alive at Christmas five years ago?'

'No. She didn't quite make it.'

'I'm sorry. I don't know. Does it matter?' He had pulled his shoes off, but he didn't get up. He straightened his back and undid his shirt cuffs.

'It doesn't, particularly. I'm just trying to think when it might have been. If I can think of some of the main things that were going on I can sort of narrow it down,' Sylvie said.

'But you don't need to do that.' He felt at his neck for his top button, struggled a bit, then absentmindedly unfastened the rest.

'I do. I can't remember otherwise. It all runs together.' She paused. Then she said, 'When you hardly know someone you remember everything, whole chunks of conversation, the different looks on their face. Even if you aren't in love with them. Though maybe you are, maybe that's a definition of it.'

'What's this got to do with anything?'

'I'm saying. At first it's all quite distinct but afterwards, I don't know when exactly, it all starts to run together and, unless you can think of markers, you can't get back.'

'Have you any idea what I was talking about?'

'I thought I had. Obviously.'

'I was asking you for your help.'

'I know. I was trying to remember.'

'Sylvie, I was trying to involve you.'

Sylvie was silent.

'I need to make decisions and I would like your help.'

'I'd like to help.'

'So. You go on about whether your mother was alive and how things run together.'

She took a deep breath. She must have missed something. He wanted them to make a decision. She needed her wits about her and they weren't there. She stared at him to see if she could find the connection she'd lost. He had stopped undressing and had put his hands on his knees and bent over, looking at the space between his feet. The familiarity and falseness that had comforted her in their embrace created fog in her head. Now he stood up and was undoing his belt. He was struggling with the fastening.

'Fuck. I've broken a nail. Where are the scissors? I must have put on weight again. Do I look as if I have?'

'Not particularly. You look fine. Nice.' She wasn't sure he did, but she said it.

'Have you got them?'

'What?'

164

'The scissors.'

'No. Was I supposed to have them?'

'Well, I just asked you for them.'

'Did you? Sorry. They're usually on the shelf in the bathroom. In the stripey pot.'

'Thanks.'

He didn't move. Neither did Sylvie. He unzipped his trousers and pulled them down, stepped out of them. He did this every night, whatever the circumstances, however inopportune the moment. Sylvie thought, I wish I were married to a man who, when he was angry, stayed fully clothed. He would run out of the house or go and sit and sulk in another room. She wouldn't have minded which. Paul always carried on getting ready for bed. Past a certain point, it's no good sleeping with someone, actually sleeping, you just see how babyish they are. She'd forgotten how well the mixture worked, amorousness and going to sleep; the other head so close by in the dark. She couldn't understand how she'd managed to forget the feelings. But the sleep was stronger, earlier.

She pulled herself from daydreaming. 'Do you want to go back to talking about Christmases?' she asked.

'This Christmas, not Christmases. Not especially. I'd say the subject was dead. Though it would have been useful to discuss it with you.'

She was sure he had been talking about the past. Now he was saying he hadn't been.

She took her shoes off by wedging one foot against the other for leverage. She was still standing up. Then she put them back on.

'It seems very hot in here. Do you think something's gone wrong with the thermostat?'

165

He didn't reply.

'I thought, before I went away, that the pipes were making different noises, as though they were just heating and heating up,' she said.

'It's turned colder.'

'I suppose so.'

'Get someone to come in and look if you think something's the matter.'

Paul was undressed now and in his pyjamas. He went into the bathroom leaving the door open. She heard him pee and flush the toilet, turn the tap on, brush his teeth, spit, turn the tap off. He came out again. He evidently wasn't bothering to wash.

'Aren't you going to get ready for bed?' he said.

'Soon. I'm being slow for some reason. Sorry.'

'Do you want to know what I was talking about?'

'Of course. I said so.'

'Christmas is on a Monday. So Saturday and Sunday are a problem. They need some thought. The working week, leading up to them, won't be any trouble.'

Sylvie could see it. The lack of trouble. The place decked out: a lighted tree in the hall, a real one that smelled of the forest and needed sweeping up after twice a day, Chinese lanterns and berries in every vase, red candles on each table, the brass and the glassware made to shine. Felix and the other young ones wanting to party and taking time off. Lucien, overtired at school, catching something. Respectable sounding office dinners catered for. Other clients given seasonal adult meals, neither ceremonial nor symbolic.

'No, we're used to that,' she said.

'It's the weekend,' he said. 'Three days in a row. Saturday. Christmas Eve. Christmas. The guests

166

who are staying are booked into all three of them. I've only just realised that's how it works out. It's usually you who spots things like that.'

'I see what you mean. It's not natural like Easter,' Sylvie said.

'Easter?'

'A three day event. Isn't it?'

'What's that got to do with it?'

'It takes three days. Though, I agree, there's a lull in the middle between Good Friday and Easter Day. No one bothers about the descent into hell. Going to the garden centre or the races doesn't count, I wouldn't have thought.'

'Sylvie.'

'We could try something different?' she said.

'Like what?'

'I don't know. A pianist, a string quartet, theme nights. Christmas 1914, for the theme night.'

'There's no need to be flippant.'

'I didn't mean to be. I was just trying to think of something. Everyone could exchange cigarettes.'

'It wasn't a serious suggestion, though, was it? You weren't actually being helpful. You never like that type of thing at the best of times, certainly not at present.'

'At present,' she repeated.

'In your present frame of mind.'

Sylvie let this go. She thought, what would Maude say. Maude would say that the variations should be culinary, that this would give scope to Paul's creativity. She would discuss with him where his ideas came from, until he had one. She would follow each through to completion, asking supportive questions about staying power and appearance. She would look entirely sincere and

167

neither of them would smile. This wasn't a solution, it was normality warmed up. The clients would pay a bit more than usual and the colour palette would be festive. If this was the solution, then there had never been a problem. Sylvie couldn't say what Maude would have said.

'Will your parents come over on all three days?' she asked.

'I've no idea. What's that got to do with it?'

'I don't know. I just wondered.'

'I imagine they'll come on Christmas Day. I haven't heard that this year's any different from usual. They'll cater for my brother on Christmas Eve. They might like to come on the Saturday too, to give them a break.'

She took her watch off and put it down on the bedside table. Half past midnight. Yvette and Gilles, no Yvette and Gilles, Yvette and Gilles. Paul got into his side of the bed and switched off his light, lay with his face towards the room, away from where she would be once she got in. No more conversation. The other lights were a reproach so Sylvie turned them off. There was enough brightness from the bathroom for her to see by and she already saw too much. Perhaps she could say what Maude would have said. She must make an effort. But her memory was of something grotesque and exaggerated, not a particular script. She doubted that she had used real words to herself a few moments ago. She would have to find new ones.

'Paul. Are you asleep?'

'No.'

'Do you want to talk some more about planning Christmas.'

'Not particularly.'

'You've done it so many times.' This wasn't what she'd meant to say.

Paul didn't say anything.

'You have to find a way of making it different. That you can get excited about. You're good at that.' This was more like Maude.

'Thanks.'

Sylvie said nothing.

'So are you,' Paul said.

'What?'

'Good at making things different. You make them utterly bizarre.'

'I don't know what you mean.'

Paul rolled half a turn and stared at the ceiling. 'I talk to you in a perfectly straightforward way and you talk complete crap back.' He turned on his side again. 'Oh, for Christ's sake, let me sleep. I try to talk to you like an adult and give you good advice. You don't take it.'

'What advice do you give me?'

'You know what I'm talking about.'

She didn't. He might have felt as if he was giving her good advice, but he wasn't.

'I did take it,' she said.

Paul stayed silent.

'I went to see Joyce.'

Paul rolled on his back again and half sat up, resting on his elbows.

'Who the hell is Joyce?'

Sylvie said nothing.

'Well?'

'I didn't mean to say anything. It was a stupid thing to say. Forget it.'

'Sylvie. Who is Joyce?'

'A medium. A spiritualist.' She paused. 'You said, go and see a fucking medium, then.'

Paul drew in his breath and collapsed onto his back. 'Sylvie, I need to sleep. I'm not going to be able to get to sleep. But I'm going to try.' He turned on his side again, away from her. 'And sometime soon, maybe tomorrow, we're going to have to have a serious talk about Lucien.'

'Lucien?'

'I said I don't want to talk anymore.'

'But you can't suddenly say that and not expect to say any more. Is something the matter with him?'

Paul shifted deeper into the bed.

'Paul. You can't do this. I'm his mother.'

'Quite.'

'Is he worried about something. Paul, you have to tell me.'

'Sylvie, shut up. Of course he's worried about something. We're all fucking worried about something. You go away. You do nothing. Sorry, you don't do nothing, you go and see Joyce. You come back. You don't say, hullo, I'm back. You say nothing. That's how you want it. All right. Now shut up.'

'What about Maude?'

Paul pulled his knees up under the duvet, his rounded form underneath, cocooned and exculpated as a foetus.

Sylvie went across the room and turned the bathroom light off. She shouldn't have let the nights come one after another like this. There should be an extra twelve hours of daylight, or an honorary night, a sort of white tent of bedclothes with no thoughts in it. She should have stopped off

170

at a hotel by the motorway, drunk a bottle of wine and stuck her head under the pillow.

She pretended that's what she had done, though she was entirely sober. She took her clothes off one by one, making a neat pile of them on the hotel chair.

CHAPTER SEVEN

The next morning Sylvie didn't get up. Paul went in the bathroom without speaking. He came out again and left the room. She heard Lucien's voice quite close on the other side of the door but he didn't come in. She heard the noise of the vacuum cleaner in the distance, then nearer, going backwards and forwards, bumping against the skirting boards, then away again. She heard Lucien and Natalie talking. After that it was quiet.

Later Paul came in and sat on the bed. She knew he was there but she didn't open her eyes to look at him. He talked to her but she didn't listen. He carried on talking and rested his hand over hers though it was under the bedclothes.

Some time afterwards she wondered what he had said. The door was shut and he had gone. She wished she'd spoken to him. If he'd sat beside her first thing she'd have liked it. That would have been the best moment for him to be there. She might have been able to get up and the day might have been ordinary. Then she stopped wondering.

Sylvie opened her eyes. The curtains were drawn open and she could see the pale blank squares of window. The room was full of pasty winter afternoon light. She stretched out for her watch. It said ten past two. She pulled herself up and sat on the edge of the bed. There was a full cup of tea on the table next to her. She dipped a finger in it. Then she lay back and slept again.

The next time she opened her eyes it was dark. Her watch said five to five. She got up and went and stood over the bathroom basin. She saw her face flannel. She filled the basin with hot water, immersed the flannel in it and wrung it until no more drops came out of it. She rubbed it over her face, as if it wasn't her own face she was touching and the sensation was warm and rough, hardly damp at all. She dried herself with a towel. Her clothes were in a pile on the chair but, as she picked them up to put on, she realised they were yesterday's clothes. She shut the curtains without looking out, turned the light on and got clean things out of the cupboard. Her dressing was slow and deliberate and she was aware of the touch of each garment as she put it on, and the difference of one from another, and the order they came in. When she'd finished she slipped her shoes on. They felt odd, so she looked down to check they were hers, then she left the bedroom. Having taken a few steps along the passage, she remembered that she hadn't brushed her hair. She went back and found her hairbrush, pulled it through her hair without looking in the mirror; first the back, then the right side then the left. She went out for the second time and this time she reached the internal door that separated their apartment from the restaurant. She found it hard to make progress, but her legs moved perfectly. She walked along until she got to the bend and continued past four closed doors. The colours and shapes in the hall seemed shockingly clear after the dimly lit corridor. A man and a woman were standing in front of the fire.

'I like it here,' the woman said, in English. She was English. Her clothes fitted her, as tight as a plum skin, but the rings on her fingers were loose. She was fiddling with them, rubbing her hands.

'I wish we'd booked in for Christmas. It's cosy.'

'Is it cold out?' Sylvie said, 'I haven't been outside yet today.'

'Haven't you?' the woman said. She stared at Sylvie. 'I don't suppose you need to.'

Sylvie didn't know how to reply. There was one small part of her mind that functioned, and it seemed to be a part that she couldn't rely on. Everything was loud and bright. She went across to the desk and eased herself into her chair.

'I love a fire to look at,' the woman said. 'A fire, or a baby in the room. You can't keep your eyes off them.' She paused. 'It's all on tap, isn't it? I had a friend who ran a place like this. It was all there, all laid on, you name it: food, booze, gym, jacuzzi, pool, people running round after you, cooking and cleaning. She didn't even make her own bed. She left it though. The life.'

Neither Sylvie nor the man spoke.

'She did. She was a friend of mine.'

'Who?' the man said.

'Francesca.'

'I didn't know she was in the hotel business,' he said.

'You're not saying she wasn't, are you, because she was.'

'I wasn't saying anything.'

'I know why you think that.' She paused. 'I know because I'd have thought the same if she hadn't been a friend of mine. Her face doesn't fit, does it? You tell me why it doesn't and then I'll tell you if I agree.'

'She's more your friend,' the man said.

'Go on,' the woman said.

'I don't know.'

'Go on. I mean, would you say she's no good with people?'

'Something like that. Disorganised.'

'You're right. That's not why she left, though.' She turned to Sylvie. 'Are you English?'

'Partly,' said Sylvie.

'I knew you were. I can always tell. It's a nice place you've got here. Peaceful. You get the key and take the things upstairs,' she said to the man. 'It's all right if I sit here, isn't it?'

'Fine,' said Sylvie.

'Eleven's the number,' the man said. 'Room eleven.'

Sylvie looked at the numbers on the board behind the desk and after a few seconds, handed him the key. He went up the stairs and the woman settled down in the armchair. She stretched her feet towards the fire.

'It was man trouble. *He's* not interested in that sort of thing. Are you married to a Frenchman?'

'Yes,' said Sylvie.

'What's that like?'

'All right,' said Sylvie.

The woman nodded. 'Sometimes he's hard to talk to.' She looked up at the staircase. 'But that's not unusual,' she said.

Paul came in through the door of the dining room. He stopped when he saw Sylvie. The woman looked at him casually and turned back to the fire.

'Sylvie.' Paul went over and leant across her desk. Sylvie didn't move. 'You shouldn't be here,' he said. He talked quietly, close to her face, conscious of the client in the armchair.

'I'm fine,' said Sylvie.

'Please,' he said.

'Don't worry about me.'

'You shouldn't have got up.'

'I'm fine.'

'Let me come back with you.'

'No,' said Sylvie.

'I can't cope with you in the restaurant.'

'That's all right,' said Sylvie. 'You won't need to.'

'I can't stay with you.'

'I know.'

'Everything's organised. You don't need to be here.'

'Where's Lucien?'

'My mother came to collect him. I told you everything's sorted.'

'I'll just sit at the desk.'

'Please, Sylvie.'

'I'll sit here. I'd rather.'

'Don't move then. Unless you go back to bed. Don't try to do anything. Sylvie are you listening to me?'

'Yes.'

'What did I say?'

Sylvie said nothing. Paul put one hand on her shoulder and looked at her face, then he went out.

'What was that all about?' the woman said.

'I don't know,' said Sylvie. 'Too many things. I've been in bed all day and he's saying I should go back there.'

'He's your husband?'

'Yes,' said Sylvie.

'No one else would stick his nose in your face and talk to you like that.' She glanced up the stairs again. *'He's* not my husband.' She stroked her left sleeve. 'Do you like my jacket?'

'Yes,' said Sylvie. 'It's a good colour.'

'You dress French, don't you? I couldn't manage that. The underwear and everything. I haven't got the concentration. It suits you. But I'm not sure it *is* you.' She went on, 'Your jumper's the wrong way round.'

Sylvie felt for the label, just under where her necklace should have been. 'I put it on in a hurry. No. No, I didn't, I put it on slowly.' She started to get her arms out of the sleeves.

The telephone rang.

'You don't mind my telling you, do you?'

'No,' said Sylvie. She pulled her jersey right off, turned it round and put it back on again.

'You've got nice skin,' the woman said in a matter of fact way. 'You'd better answer the phone.'

Sylvie picked it up. It was Yvette.

'That's not you, is it, darling?'

'Yes, it is me,' Sylvie said.

'Where are you?'

'In the usual place. I'm in the entrance hall, sitting at my desk.'

'Paul's not about, by any chance, is he, darling. I'd just like a little word with him.'

'He's in the kitchen. He seemed rather pressed. I can give him a message.'

'Just ask him to give me a moment, would you, darling?'

'Is it something urgent then?'

Yvette hummed into the telephonc and wouldn't commit herself.

'But you can't tell me about it, is that it?'

Sylvie listened to Yvette's circumlocutions. She wasn't speaking straight into the mouthpiece. Gilles was chipping in and she was giving him

177

instructions. Suddenly Sylvie heard commotion and crying. Yvette said, 'Don't worry, darling. I'll call you back,' and put the phone down.

'You weren't here yesterday when we arrived. It was another woman,' her companion said.

Sylvie sat there. Her patience felt a burden, more like stoicism. The woman by the fire was looking at her. The telephone rang again. It was sooner than Sylvie had hoped for. But it was Maude.

'Oh, Sylvie, you're up.'

'Yes, I'm up. Why is that surprising? I wasn't back late yesterday.'

'Paul said you were rather fed up and had had a lie in.'

'Did he? Well, I'm fine thank you.' Sylvie's heard her own replies as abrupt. Maude, at the other end was sounding euphonic, as if she were trying to warm up a difficult language class. She said something had cropped up which meant she couldn't come in and she hoped she could touch base with Paul.

'He's in the kitchen. I'll put you through if you like, but he seemed pretty busy. Is something the matter? Nothing serious, I hope.'

Someone at the other end was listening. Alain.

'No, it's some stupid muddle with dates. I feel really bad about it. You've both got so much on, now we're into December and the Christmas parties are starting,' she said.

'Don't worry, Maude. It can't be helped.'

'You will tell Paul, won't you?' she said.

'Yes, of course I'll tell him.'

Paul came through the dining room door.

'He's just walked in. I'll tell him now. Bye.' She

178

put the telephone down. 'That was Maude. She can't come this evening.'

'But she's got to. She said she was going to.'

'There's no need to sound so annoyed.'

'What explanation did she give?'

Sylvie shrugged her shoulders.

'Why didn't you let me speak to her?'

His annoyance had found its right object.

'I was right here,' he said. 'You were talking to her as I walked in. It would have been the simplest thing to put her on. Why didn't you do that?'

'It wouldn't have made any difference.'

'That's got nothing to do with it. You're stupid. Wilful; like a child.'

Sylvie thought, this wilfulness that they don't like is the strong part. I just haven't got it quite right yet. It's when I manage, and put on a brave face, that I'm weak.

'What's the matter with her anyway?' Paul said.

'Something minor and domestic. It didn't sound too terrible.'

'She can come in then. I'll call her back.'

'Alain will answer,' Sylvie said.

'Sorry?'

'I wouldn't bother. Alain will answer.'

'Why should that be a problem?'

The telephone rang again.

'I imagine he stopped her from coming,' said Sylvie.

Paul picked the receiver up with a flourish from the other side of the desk.

'Hullo.' He sounded combative.

'Oh, it's you Mummy. No, I'm not cross.'

'No, just a bit concerned. The usual sort of thing.'

'Yes, she is up. Up but . . .'

'I've no idea. I wouldn't say so. No.'

'Sorry?'

'Is he? That's not like him.'

'No, I'm not suggesting it's your fault. You're always so good with him.'

'He'll calm down soon. Have you given him something to eat?'

'No, of course I know you wouldn't neglect him.'

'Hasn't he?'

'Shall I talk to him?'

'Won't he?'

'If there's no alternative. You'll have to.'

'No, I'm sure you've tried everything.'

'We'll just have to, won't we?'

'I'm not sounding like anything.'

'Well, I didn't mean to.'

'All right. I'll see you shortly.'

Paul put the telephone down.

'That was my mother.'

'What's happened?' said Sylvie.

'She's bringing Lucien back.'

'He's ill?'

'No. He wants to see you.'

'Well, I want to see him.'

'Apparently he's been crying.' Paul stared at Sylvie without emotion. 'I haven't liked today,' he said. 'Or yesterday evening.'

He went out.

*   *   *

The woman got up from the armchair.

'I'm sorry I was here for all that,' she said. 'I was going to go, but then I thought it would be better to

180

sit tight. I'll go up now. He's probably fallen asleep. He does that when I'm out of the way. Cat naps. I think I must tire him out.'

'Don't go,' said Sylvie. 'If you don't mind staying a bit longer, I'd like you to.'

'All right,' said the woman.

'Talk to me,' said Sylvie. 'Tell me about Francesca.'

'You're interested in her, are you? What do you want to know?'

'Anything,' said Sylvie.

'We were teenage together. Not school. She went to hers on a bus. We used to see each other at dance classes and hanging about the Marina. She was lovely. All over the place, though. I never thought she'd settle, not easily.' She stopped. 'Are you sure you want to hear about someone you don't know?'

'Yes,' said Sylvie.

'This entrepreneur hippy type fell for her. Well, that bit wasn't surprising, but the next I heard was that he'd set her up in business with him in a leisure complex in Cornwall. That did surprise me. She stuck it for five years. Then, one evening, she left a note in the hotel swimming pool, one word a sheet, all floating on the water. They had a hundred karmic astrologers staying there. She wasn't good with the New Agers. Not on their wavelength. She ran away to a man she'd met on the beach; hitched a lift to Cardiff. She didn't need to. She had her own car. That's what she's like. Jeff, her partner, caught the bits of paper in the net they used for getting wasps and leaves out. He threw them away without going to the bother of working out the message. She found that out later.'

'She didn't tell you what she wrote?' said Sylvie.

'No,' said the woman. 'That was her all over. She said it had gone. That was the end of it.'

Sylvie didn't feel any need to ask what had happened to her. This moment of escape didn't have the status of a turning point. It wasn't something with consequences, something to live up to. She could see Francesca, as if she were standing in front of her. She had very particular looks, the sort that get a woman in and out of trouble without her knowing why. She could also see the message, the feeling of it anyway; brave and flawed. Francesca might even have missed out a crucial word.

'Is anything else wrong with me besides my jersey?' she asked.

She felt she needed to exert herself and this was all she could think of.

'Let's look at you,' said the woman. 'I'd say your hair isn't sitting right. It's tidy but sort of going in the wrong direction. Hair's a spiral, isn't it? You can't argue with the way it's meant to go. And you're not wearing any make-up. Do you want me to fix it for you?'

'I haven't got anything with me,' said Sylvie.

'Borrow mine,' said the woman. 'I always travel with a full kit of slap. There's a ladies down here, isn't there? I'll come with you.'

Sylvie was about to say she could manage on her own, but, when she got up, she said, 'Thank you.' She felt unsteady and she needed the woman's company. They walked across the hall and along the passage. The woman held the door open for her and then propped it open with one of her high-heeled shoes. There was only just room for the two

182

of them and hot air came out in gusts from a vent. Sylvie noticed that Natalie had kept it gleaming; no hair in the plug hole, or wound round the soap, to put the clients off their dinners. She thought her companion might insist on helping, but she didn't. She offered the cosmetic bag as if it were a packet of sweets. Sylvie dipped into it tentatively and applied the other woman's colours. She used her hairbrush. It wasn't as uncomfortable as it might have been. More like borrowing clothes in an emergency than getting in a stranger's bath water. She concentrated and because the woman was looking at her impartially, with interest, not searchingly, she made her face in the mirror relax into someone she recognised. There I am, she thought. She put the towel she'd used in the basket and realigned the laundered ones into a pile of white folds.

*   *   *

Lucien was pale but otherwise perfect. The marks of hysterical crying had been smoothed from his face. He came in from the cold and dark, holding his grandmother's hand as if they had had a nice uneventful day together. He remembered what had happened and how he had behaved, and now he was here, back at home, making an unscheduled return. He had an air of someone who made no connection between the two. Nothing personal, anyway.

'He's all smiles now,' Yvette said, inclined to be spiteful. She liked to be known to cope in a crisis. And although she was relieved that the appalling noise had hiccupped to an end she felt absurd walking in with this obedient child. She kept glancing at Sylvie, wondering what was different about her. Sylvie wanted to say, my friend has made my face up, which is why, although tired, your daughter-in-law looks, somehow, more vivid.

'I'm sorry you've had a rough time,' said Sylvie.

'It didn't matter to me, darling,' said Yvette. 'I just felt so sorry for him, getting himself into such a state for no good reason.'

'Never mind,' said Sylvie.

She knew that Yvette supposed that if Lucien was able to be calm and happy now he could have been calm and happy an hour ago and remained at his grandparents'. Her mother-in-law probably supposed the same about her. If she was up now, why couldn't she have got up this morning like everyone else who wasn't ill or on shift work? It bothered her herself. She had lapsed and so had Lucien.

CHAPTER EIGHT

The three of them sat round the table in the tiny dining room of their flat. It was half past five on Christmas morning and the only time they would be on their own together. Sylvie and Paul had both got to bed at two o'clock. They were tired with a tiredness that wouldn't shift but could be cajoled by hot coffee. The room was the same as it was in the evening; the curtains drawn, the lamp turned on, the furniture identically set out, but the light and the colours had a different quality, harsher and more sickly. Lucien had woken early but wasn't the cause of this inconvenient breakfast. He knew he wasn't and made the most of it.

'Everyone in my class will be up now,' he said.

'No they won't,' said Sylvie.

'Yes they will,' said Lucien. 'They'll make their parents get up.'

'Bernard possibly will, but none of the others,' said Sylvie.

'Bernard won't,' said Lucien. 'He never wakes up.'

'He won't have had such great presents, anyway,' said Paul.

'He already got judo lessons for his birthday. He won't get anything else.'

It was too soon for conversation and Sylvie and Paul were joined together in adult resistance to it. Across the table she saw a man exposed by the time, the day, the energy of his son, the circumstances that had brought him to this point. She knew she was equally blighted. And beyond the

185

intervening door was the narcosis of the restaurant. The sleeping clients, oblivious of their surroundings, but lying in wait for them. They'd booked in advance and had expectations. They'd be dreaming of races and chases and water and falling and work and love, but they'd wake up thinking of breakfast laid on clean tablecloths and what there might be for lunch. The place would be in darkness apart from the dim corridor lighting and the red glow of the emergency connection on the hall telephone.

'Are you all right?' said Paul, ignoring whatever Lucien was saying. 'We were late last night.'

'Not too bad,' said Sylvie. 'Are you?'

She could still do it; begin days and get through them. She hadn't known whether she would be able to. It was Christmas and she'd reached it. When she had got up from her bed three weeks ago she had forced herself not to get back in and since then she had managed to stay in the daytime world. She had worked without stopping, confined to the building. At night she disappeared into a tunnel. She and Paul sheltered each other without being companionable. Sylvie thought how strange it was that their observances carried on. There were no days off so they hadn't eaten together but they talked to one another and synchronised arrangements. They had made love from time to time in a way that was neutral; not as a necessity, like drinking a glass of water from thirst, more as a reflex, like eating bread and butter that happened to be on the table. Their support of each other was partly professional, almost sophisticated. They were fully booked again this year. Saturday, Sunday, Monday. Both weeks either side. All the beds and all the tables. Her autumn advertising had paid off. She'd arranged that before George died. The weather was terrible; murky, typical northern French. The sky never changed from day to day.

Paul, Yvette and Gilles were being careful with her. They knew that Christmas was a difficult time for anyone who had had trouble during the course of the year, bereavement, divorce, that sort of thing, and that the later on in the year the event happened, the more difficult the festive season was likely to be. They remained themselves, of course, but Sylvie was aware of their efforts. Paul himself was looking fragile having, temporarily, lost Maude. She seemed to be under curfew. And then there was Lucien.

Paul had had his talk with her about him. He had avoided bedtime, choosing a quiet moment in the hall when guests weren't obviously passing. He didn't say she hadn't been a fit mother and needed to pull herself together. He didn't complain of her absences. One thing got substituted for another and he said that it seemed a bit tough on Lucien living in a restaurant, having all those extra people around; that it wasn't like an ordinary family Christmas. Lucien was old enough to know that they weren't the same as other people. They needed to make sure he wasn't missing out. He had had wonderful Christmases, as a child. He wanted it to be the same for Lucien. Sylvie let Paul talk to her about it, realising he was worrying about something else. She said she didn't think Lucien had quite got to the stage of knowing his family wasn't typical. What his parents did had the status of the essential services. Of course, it was the case that, once the clients had arranged to come to them at Christmas, there was no going back. They had chosen to come to them, rather than book Nice or Martinique or do an enormous shop at the supermarket. They couldn't let them down. She agreed they weren't the same as other people. She didn't want to dismiss it. So, she and Paul were kind to each other, but the kindness was another layer of skin.

She talked to Lucien. She told him to pretend that they were on a boat, becalmed in monotonous seascape. The people who came to the restaurant couldn't go ashore, so he should try to make them feel at home. They couldn't escape to the kitchen, to cook or wash up, and they had to get on with strangers. He wasn't particularly impressed by the comparison. He'd never been on a boat, not even a cross Channel ferry. But Paul seemed satisfied that she was making an effort.

At six o'clock, Paul left to work in the kitchen. Sylvie poured herself some more coffee and counted the hours ahead. After tidying up, she and Lucien shut the door to their apartment and walked down the corridor. She made him whisper but she let him rearrange the cards that were hanging on strings in the hall. They were mostly connected with the business; large and traditional, or large and fashionably untraditional. There was one from Don. The computer was switched off and the telephone was silent. She moved around the dining room making small adjustments, laying the tables that weren't going to be used for breakfast, with lunch-time cutlery and glasses. Apart from the rain, there were no sounds from outside. The farm vehicles stood idle. No cars or lorries went by on the main road. They would have to travel a long way to find any life. The nearby town would be deserted, shuttered up. The shops with their tills covered, fishmongers mopped dry, butchers bleached clean, the florist empty of all but silk flowers, Jacques' bar unlit. She thought, if I don't sit down, I shall get everything done.

At eight o'clock the hum of a guest's television reached the hall, the first of the day. Soon afterwards, a man came out of a ground-floor bedroom with a dog in his arms and wagged his finger at Lucien, before slipping out of the front door. It was just beginning to get light.

The older clients were the first down. Retired couples, in pairs, or with friends. They had dressed carefully from the limited supply of clothes in their suitcases, some rather smartly, so that they wouldn't have to change again later. There was always someone who felt she had made the wrong choice of Sunday best and whose stay was spoilt because of it. Last year it had been a woman in a knitted suit with fur trimming. Something about it had made her uncomfortable. She had complained about the chair she was sitting on and after Sylvie had changed it, she had asked for the heating to be turned down.

As they entered the dining room, they exchanged Christmas greetings tentatively, the English making an effort with their French, or simply smiling. Sylvie had time to talk to them as she filled up their cups with tea or coffee. They mentioned their families. They didn't want other people to think they hadn't got any. Their children and grandchildren were, exceptionally, on winter sports' holidays. Or, they were all going to celebrate together at their daughter's fiftieth in February. Lucien survived until the first well-meaning question about his presents and then ran away.

*   *   *

George never spent Christmas with Sylvie. He stayed in London. He spoke to them all on the telephone on Christmas morning and she didn't get in touch with him or hear from him again until they exchanged letters early in January. English post always seized up for a week or more. And in the years after she had left home and before her mother died, Eve and George spent the holiday on their own together. So she didn't associate him with Christmas. She and Paul worked.

She remembered the letter she had written to him last year. Maybe not the exact words, but the gist of it. She had read it, along with the others, as she knelt on the sitting room floor in his flat. Apart from topical details, such as the knitted suit, it could have been describing any year in the previous five, though Lucien grew bigger, the business became more successful, they all got older. She had given George the flavour of it. His letters, back to her, were the same; true, but partial. His painstaking descriptions of what he'd cooked for himself, his assumed laboriousness and incompetence, his accounts of Boxing Day with Don and Judith, his subsequent escapes to fresh air and the pub, were exaggerated for her benefit. He missed out his bravery in doing any of it without Eve and the distortions he had had to accommodate; not just the emptiness of his wife not being there, but the deformed shape that had taken her place. He and Sylvie had told each

190

other what was acceptable and bearable. This year she had no one to tell.

CHAPTER NINE

In England it didn't stop raining. It eased off on the afternoon of December 25 without giving up altogether and English families set out to stretch their legs or get a breath of fresh air, letting the brain contract out and the day itself take them for a walk as though they were dogs.

Jerry set off down the lane with Gillian at three o'clock. No one else would come out with them. It was probably the third year they had been unaccompanied. In previous years either Nicholas or Alice would agree to go, as long as the other didn't. This was also the period when his aunt would have been able to make it limb-wise, but stayed indoors to keep his mother company. There were years before that, when both his mother and aunt could still make it, but Alice wouldn't go because the grown-ups outnumbered the children and occasionally talked among themselves. These were blocks of time and were broken up by particular years when individual family members dropped out through illness, and sometimes, depending who they were, needed someone, usually Gillian, to attend to them. There must have been a time when all six of them went on the walk together but Jerry couldn't recall it. He didn't think of Christmas from one December to the next and then the sense of dozens of them came to him at once, as if they all happened in an eternal present and overlay each other, like strips of negative in old photograph packets. If he had had time to get to the bottom of the pile he'd have found the Holy

Family.

'If we got there well in advance, say three or four days before, we could warm the house up.' Gillian paused. 'We'd take the food but we'd have to keep an eye on the sell-by dates.'

'What did you buy it for then?' Jerry said.

'Sorry, Jerry?'

'Don't worry. They err on the side of caution. We'll have eaten it all in a few hours' time. The kids'll keep it down. And the old dears. They're more robust than they look. They never throw up at Christmas. Flu, yes. Heavy colds, yes. Nothing gastric.'

'You're wrong, actually. Don't you remember Alice?' Gillian said.

'When was that?'

'I don't know. She was younger. Yes, I do. Exactly. It was the year we decided to cut out presents between the adults.'

'How did that work?' he said.

'It didn't. Everyone gave to everyone else, the same as usual. I suppose the presents were a bit smaller. But no, no they weren't. I remember thinking it would be cheaper, but it wasn't. Not at all. And Nicholas didn't give anything to anyone.'

'That wouldn't have worried him.'

'It didn't. He said I'd told him the wrong thing.'

'Just out of interest, why did you buy stuff that was going off? I mean, it doesn't matter. But no doubt you had a reason,' he said.

'Nothing important. You weren't listening to what I was saying, actually.'

A puddle stretched across the lane, large enough to ripple as the wind caught it.

'Shall we risk it? The gravelly bit in the middle's

disappeared. You didn't change your shoes,' said Gillian.

'It's always bad here. There's a bit to the left which is usually safe. There, by that clump.'

'That black bit? I don't think so.'

'No, not that, further over.'

'It would be a change though, wouldn't it?' said Gillian.

'What?'

'To go to the Vosges another year. I suppose we could buy the food once we got there. But I don't know the butcher.'

'You don't know the fellow here, do you?'

'Neil. Yes. Yes I do. I mean the meat he gives me isn't record breaking. I usually go to Tescos. Anyway, that's only one thing. There are the beds. Alice and Nicholas would be up past midnight.'

'Would they? Why?'

'If they're sleeping in the sitting room on camp beds. I'm just thinking aloud. No, it won't work.'

'Why aren't they in their own beds?'

'It wouldn't *feel* like Christmas, is what I really think, and we'd all be shut up together with awful weather outside and nowhere to escape to.'

'Sounds familiar.'

'Don't be silly Jerry, this is home and it *feels* like Christmas. And your mother and Aunt Lou would miss Church.'

'They'd be there would they? Yes, I suppose they would. That explains the bed situation. Al gave me that car sticker, do you remember, saying Go to Church now, beat the Christmas rush. Quite funny, really. She can't have been more than five.'

'You didn't think it was very funny at the time. It was Valentine's day. You were rather offended.

194

She'd drawn hearts all over the envelope. And the other thing is, the oven is actually quite titchy and there's nowhere to warm the plates.'

'It has its charms. The back of beyond. I slept incredibly well when I was there in November.'

'I suppose, one thing we *could* do, would be to stay in an hotel on the way down for Christmas itself and then go to the Vosges for the in-between bit and New Year. I mean, it doesn't matter if New Year isn't much to write home about. Or the bit in between.'

'Where are you thinking of going? Somewhere simple near Gatwick, or one of those palazzo kind of places outside Calais?'

'What was the place you stayed at on the way back last time?' she said. 'You never really told me about it.'

'In fact, New Year *does* matter. More than Christmas. It's symbolic. You can't intend to start off on the wrong foot. I mean, if it goes wrong, it goes wrong, but you can't intend it. Not even you, Gill.'

'So, what was it called?'

'God, I can't remember that. Something beginning with at the.'

'At the?'

'Yes, you know. French. Au moulin de la something. Only it wasn't that.'

'Was the food any good?'

'Not bad. Not amazing, as in, amazing, but not bad. He'll never be a star. The chef, that is. He was a bit of a time waster. However, it was incredibly well run. Up there with the best. The woman who did it—ran it—was one of those invisible types. You didn't notice her. I mean I couldn't describe her to you now. But she made everything kind of glide. You weren't aware particularly *what* she was doing but she gave you exactly what you needed before you knew you needed it.'

'She sounds a paragon. One of those super efficient, buttoned-up French women.'

'She wasn't actually. She was odd. Conventional, but odd. Nice looking.'

'You said you couldn't describe her.'

'I can't, really.'

'So, what was so special about her.'

'For instance. Some poor sod at the next table died. In the middle of his retirement party. She coped. He was lucky to have her around.'

'Who?'

'The fellow who pegged it.'

'Why?'

'She could have been anyone. A martinet. A ratbag. She sort of shielded him. I didn't even know what had happened. We could all do with someone like that around at the end. It's more likely to be like that, isn't it? Random, like that.'

'Than what?'

'I don't know. Nearest and dearest round the bed. And would you want them?'

'He wouldn't have known she was his guardian angel.'

'He might have done. Unconsciously.'

'How mystical. Have you seen her since?'

'Gillian, she lives in some obscure part of France. She'll be there now leaning over the Christmas diners, draining the last drops of lunch-time wine into their glasses. They'll be too pissed to appreciate her.'

'I thought you'd stopped all that sort of thing,

Jerry.'

*　　　*　　　*

The house was silent when Jerry and Gillian got back from their walk. Jerry went into the drawing room and sat down in a spare chair that wasn't his usual one because Aunt Lou was sitting in that. This one wasn't as comfortable. Luckily there would soon be tea and fruit cake and this would run into champagne and dinner and the day would speed up and be over. Alice had piled up cushions at the end of the sofa and was pretending to be asleep because she wouldn't play cards with Nicholas. She and everyone else thought she was being unusually selfless in resisting passively. Nicholas stared at her without blinking and hoped his gaze would pierce her eyelids. Jerry's mother started to say that Catholics don't understand hymns and he had no idea why she said that, unless he had said something about spending Christmas in France. He honestly couldn't remember saying it, or whether he said it this year, or last. Aunt Lou said it was a shame the rain had stopped them from going to church, which it hadn't. They had gone to church, all except Alice. Nicholas interrupted his great aunt and said that he had suddenly realised the point of life. No one asked him what it was. He waited for thirty seconds and said that, if you didn't remember what happened a few hours ago, you might as well be dead, so the point of life must be to remember what happened a few hours ago.

Eventually they all drank tea brewed in a proper teapot because it was a family occasion and the milk tasted slightly acidic, like French tea. There wasn't any fruit cake, they couldn't find it.

'Dad, where do you think Mum is?' Nicholas said.

'Don't bother asking, he's not listening,' Alice said.

'Why is she out in the garden?'

'She isn't.'

'She is. You can't see her. You've got your eyes closed.'

'So has Dad.'

'How do you know?'

'I can tell.'

'What's Mum doing then, if you're so clever?'

'She wouldn't be out there today.'

'Why not? What's so special about today? What day is it, Aunt Lou?'

'I don't know, darling. I'll just find my glasses.'

'It's the Incarnation, Aunt Lou,' Nicholas said.

'Where did you get that from? Just tell her it's the day before Boxing Day,' Alice said.

'It is, isn't it, Dad? What is the Incarnation?'

It was almost dark outside. Jerry opened his eyes and pulled himself up from the armchair to draw the curtains.

'A once and for all thing, without scope for repetition,' he said.

The light from behind him shone onto the garden. There were pools of water on the lawn that never drained away. The leaves that hadn't been swept up had blown into them. Gillian *was* out there. He could just make her out. She was bending down and fishing for leaves, wringing them out with her rubber gloves and putting them into a black plastic bag.

Jerry came away from the window. He stared at the fire. The ash had formed an escarpment that extended beyond the grate. It glittered with bits of unconsumed wrapping paper. He went towards the door.

'Where are you going, Dad? Are you going to open another bottle?'

'You're not, are you, Jerry?'

Gillian met him in the doorway.

'No, Gillian. I'm not.'

He came back in and sat down again.

'Where were you going, Dad?' Nicholas said. 'Would you like another piece of Turkish Delight, Gran? Shall I find you a rose one?'

CHAPTER TEN

'You look lovely, darling. She does, doesn't she, Gilles?' Yvette said.

'Thank you,' said Sylvie.

'We're so proud of you.'

'For coming back from the brink?'

'Sorry, darling, I didn't quite catch that.'

'Where is it, do you think?'

'Where's what, Sylvie?'

'Never mind. You enjoyed your dinner?'

'It was wonderful. The most wonderful dinner. As always when we come here. And all over too soon.'

'You'll be all right driving back?'

'Of course, darling. Gilles has done the enjoying for me and I'll get him back in one piece. Not that it's quite time to leave yet. We'll squeeze another few minutes out of the evening.

Yvette looked round the dining room as though she were noticing it for the first time. 'You seem to have a nice crowd here.'

'Much the same as usual.'

'I haven't spotted Maude. She usually puts in an appearance.'

'No, she's not here this evening.'

'I don't think I saw her on Saturday either, did I?'

'No.'

Yvette beamed at her. 'Well you're managing very well, darling, short handed.'

Sylvie had made the restaurant beautiful; better than ever. It was a genuine transformation. The

200

evergreens made their own deep holes of shadow; lights multiplied in every surface. Everything seemed brighter, with that brightness that glazed plates acquire when they get too hot in the oven. They brighten and then they crack.

The guests weren't leaving the dining room. They never did over Christmas. Usual reasons for wanting bed didn't apply: boredom, exhaustion, desire, a good book, connectedness with the next day, a fit sense of the end of this one. Paul came across to his parents' table. He had already made his patronal round. This was more informal. Yvette liked being incognito, as if she were a film star in dark glasses and a wig. She knew who she was, the mother of the chef, but pretended no one else did. A fat man wearing a bow tie had said what a nice child Lucien was and she hadn't been able to resist leaning across and saying, 'That's my grandson.' Lucien had stayed up, sitting with his grandparents, until after the pudding, then Yvette had whisked him into bed. That was the arrangement they had come to. It was the first year he had stayed up.

'Darling,' Yvette said, 'we were just saying how good Lucien was. A happy little boy. Not the easiest situation, sharing his family with all and sundry. He really rose to the occasion.'

Paul put his hand on Sylvie's shoulder. Yvette smiled at Gilles as if to say, that's a good sign.

'We'll set a good example, shall we, dear? If we move it might start a trend. Then Paul and Sylvie will be able to get to bed.'

Yvette bent down and rummaged in her bag for her car keys. She put them on the table by her empty coffee cup and the glass that still had wine in it, but she didn't get up. She won't leave, Sylvie thought, until she's had Paul to herself for a moment; it's a kind of superstition, like touching wood. She reached for Paul's hand and moved it from her shoulder, made her excuses and went over to a couple at the other side of the dining room. She hadn't had time to speak to them properly earlier. They were the people from Metz who had been there the night Maurice died. She was glad they had wanted to come back again.

*   *   *

After midnight people began to move. They pushed back their chairs and stood up, aware of the weight of their stomachs. But instead of nodding and leaving, as they usually did at the end of an evening, they clung together in groups. They had a belated sense that it was Christmas and they could have been one big party. It hadn't been necessary to keep themselves to themselves quite so strictly. In the remaining minutes there was no risk in being friendly.

They left the dining room, laughing and talking. Someone was whistling. The ones who had bedrooms and only the stairs to climb looked complacent. The others, who were heading for the car park, searched for their coats. Sylvie was helping them when the telephone rang. She finished fitting a woman into her mackintosh and went to answer it.

'Sylvie?'

'It's you,' she said. 'I wasn't expecting to hear from you.'

'I wasn't expecting to speak to you either,' said Jerry.

'I might not have answered. Someone else might have picked up the telephone.'

'That would have been all right. I'd have booked a room for January.'

'Are you coming, in January?'

'Not as far as I know. How has Christmas been?'

'All right so far. How has yours been?'

'It's a mad house. Nothing new to report.'

'The couple from Metz have come back again. Do you remember them?'

'No. Should I? Who are they?'

'There's no reason why you should. They were here when you were. I don't know why I said that. It just seemed a coincidence. With you calling. It isn't particularly interesting. What are you doing for the rest of the holiday?'

'Tomorrow I am taking my mother and my aunt back to their respective dwellings. That's the plan, anyway. I can tell you, it's something I do with a light heart.'

'Do they know you're talking to me? It's late.'

'I said I was going to call the house in the Vosges. In fact, I started to. I began with the code for France and then I dialled your number.'

'Who's staying there?'

'Where?'

'In the Vosges.'

'No one. I like hearing the telephone ring. I pretend I'm there. It calms me down. I need to sell it. You don't want to buy it, do you? It's a nice little hideaway.'

'No, thank you.'

'But you got back there all right, I wondered. Back to the Moselle. Are you coming to London again, at some stage?'

'No. Well, at some stage. Not yet. I have to put in some more time here.'

'Why's that?'

'To prove I'm competent.'

'You are, though. I've never met anyone so competent. Who says you're not?' He stopped and started again in a different voice. 'I'm talking to myself.'

'Sorry?'

'I said, I've got on to the continuous tone. I was dialling our house in France.' He was speaking away from the mouthpiece. A voice nearby was interrupting. 'If you hang on long enough, the ringing turns into a continuous tone. That must have happened to you, Al, when you call one of your friends and they don't answer. Never? You're all so bloody impatient. I got onto it with all my girlfriends. Shut the bloody door if you don't like it.'

'Jerry?'

'God, there's a lot to put up with at this end.'

'It sounds as if you need to put the phone down.'

'Maybe. Not yet.'

'I'd better go, I think.'

'Tell me everything you've done since you left.'

'Sorry, I'm not concentrating. There's a car revving outside.'

'Keep talking. Tell me about France. I like France. Talk to me in French.'

'Paul's parents are leaving. They've turned on their headlights and are sitting there outside the entrance. They're waiting for me to say goodbye to them.'

'What else is happening? It sounds like a party.'

'I'll have to go now. Paul's coming in from

outside.'

'I thought you were front of house and he stayed in the kitchen.'

'I've got to go.' She put the telephone down.

*   *   *

Paul came back in and got stuck for the next ten minutes, saying good night and holding the door for the clients. His words were affable but his actions and his smile became automatic with the opening and the shutting of the door. Outside it was cold and still. The entrance hall emptied.

'They were sorry not to say goodbye to you,' he said to Sylvie.

'Yvette and Gilles?'

She had known whom he meant but she couldn't summon up guilt.

'It doesn't matter,' he said.

'No,' she said. It didn't. The formula got repeated. Goodbye. And then when it was final, a real goodbye, she had missed saying it.

'You sounded weary,' he said. 'What were you thinking?'

'Nothing,' she said.

CHAPTER ELEVEN

The days between December 25 and 31 were always odd. They lacked potential. The decorations were still up, looking less glossy; the resinous smell fading. People ignored them, as they would do confetti on church steps after a wedding. They were glad to sink back into habit, recovering from Christmas but absolved from making resolutions. In the restaurant, Paul cooked food that propitiated the appetite and Sylvie asked the clients who hadn't been with them if they had had a good Christmas.

Felix had run into an open car door, in the village, and come off his bike. The owner of the car had been on his hands and knees hoovering the inside. He had laid out his rubber mats and pieces of detachable carpet and set up an arrangement with an extension lead. He wasn't pleased with the nosebleed. Felix said that the black eye, that spread from his eyebrow to below his cheekbone, and the bandaged left hand, looked worse than they were and wouldn't stop him from working. He was skint after Christmas and owed his mum money. Sylvie was glad to make a fuss of him. His eye was rather beautiful. Paul was nursing his emotions and this was less appealing. He seemed to want Sylvie's sympathy but she knew he wouldn't ask for it. He couldn't legitimately resent her either, as it was Alain who was keeping Maude at home; nothing to do with her. It left him with a limited range of demonstrable feelings. Alain's intervention was guesswork but Sylvie preferred to believe in it. It explained Paul's self pity. She experimented with the idea of mentioning Jerry. It wouldn't be a revelation, or a story, just a few airy sentences of fact, to show she was adult. Lucien, though, was always present, as Natalie wasn't there to take him off their hands. She was visiting her mother in Thionville and wouldn't be returning until the New Year and the start of the school term. Sylvie didn't want to summon up trouble and then not have the privacy to deal with it. She and Paul avoided trouble. Equilibrium would be a fancy word for where they'd got to, suggesting achievement, a fine balancing. It wasn't that.

*   *   *

On the afternoon of December 29 Sylvie took Lucien for a walk in the forest. The restaurant was stuffy and smelled of venison stew. The food itself had looked delicate, with carrot thinnings and thumb-nail size dumplings arranged round the edge of the plates like exclamation marks, but the smell was that of a hunters' feast, trapped in a genteel room. Four elderly Englishmen had eaten it and sped off on motorbikes to a First World War monument on the top of a shallow hill. Visibility wasn't good but the panoramic plan, at the top of the steps, would help them to reconstruct the various stages of the offensive. They were optimistic and liked the idea of blotting out the contemporary detail with a mist. A couple had eaten the stew and set off for Luxembourg. The car park was empty.

Lucien ran ahead into the forest, off the main path, leaving Sylvie behind. He wouldn't go far out of sight. He felt life with his feet; dead leaves and pine needles, felled trees and boggy puddles. It wasn't enough to look at them, he had to walk in or over them and it took twice as long. Sylvie kept to the track. The pines were dense on either side and deep beyond; tough and spiky, grown for use, slivers of brightness between the trunks. There seemed to be a change for the better in the level of light, now that Christmas was out of the way. It felt good to be out of doors, for its own sake, not just as escape. In the distance, where the trees almost met, were three figures, too far away to distinguish. Their coats showed up against the greens and browns. Then, as Sylvie approached, a fourth appeared, running across them, followed by a small white dog. Lucien had his eyes on the ground, he hadn't seen them.

'There's Maude,' said Sylvie when he swerved over in her direction. She was glad to have him there to say it to. There was something unnerving about approaching Maude head on. It would be several minutes before they reached one another, longer if their children dawdled. She didn't feel like waving. And if she had done, she would have to stop. She couldn't wave indefinitely. And then choosing the moment to begin smiling was awkward. She hadn't seen Maude for over three weeks. Not since she arrived back from London.

'Are those her children?' said Lucien.

Since he'd seen them he'd stuck next to her.

'Yes,' said Sylvie. 'You know them.'

'No I don't,' he said.

There was no point in arguing with him.

She had no idea whether Paul had spoken to Maude, or what they might have said to each other;

presumably they had spoken. She thought of them like that, almost breezily; prepared to tell herself the outward form of their story, but not to home in on the details. It wasn't so much that she stopped at the bedroom door, she wasn't afraid of that, as that she saw them as the naïve, speeded up characters in a silent movie. Round and round the kitchen they went, in and out of car seats, up and down the stairs, upright, prone. What had taken months for them, with gaps in between, she saw in minutes. She could even contemplate their future, now that the rapid, head-banging kisses had stopped. The most likely outcome was that they wouldn't see each other for a certain length of time, anything between a few months and a couple of years, long enough for Alain to ease off the vigilance, or find himself a mistress, and then they would again. They lived near each other and the area was depopulated. They wouldn't have reached this conclusion themselves. Lovers could thrive on uncertainty, but not mundane likelihoods.

She realised that she hadn't tried at all hard to imagine what Paul saw in Maude. She had stuck to the obvious: Maude's looks and the confidence that went with admiration—her stunning ability to be ingratiating. She hadn't looked any further. Maude waved. Sylvie thought, that's one thing about Maude, she's the sort to do things first. She waved back. It felt wrong to think about her as she approached. She tried, mentally, to change the subject.

'Why is Maude here?' said Lucien.

'For the same reason we are, I suppose. To go for a walk.'

'I don't want to play with those children.'

'You don't have to.'

'I might have to. You don't know.'

'Don't be unfriendly.'

Sylvie glanced back over her shoulder. They had passed the first foresters' track that cut across the main path. She hadn't noticed it. Between the trees she could see a narrow line of bonfire smoke rising from somewhere in the fields. But the line was getting finer. They'd come further than she'd thought.

'Hi,' said Maude, from a few paces away. 'You're bored with the Christmas presents too, are you? The novelty has definitely worn off. We're collecting pine-cones, aren't we troops? Hi Lucien.'

The white dog snuffled round their feet.

'We just wanted some fresh air,' said Sylvie. It was a prissy thing to say, but Maude looked and sounded as if they had met in a department store. She seemed, in spite of talking of the pine-cones, not to recognise that they were out of doors.

'Tell Sylvie what we've got.' As no one spoke, she carried on. 'We've got two lovely kittens, haven't we? I've been trying to bond them with the dog. It's not going swimmingly. Give Lucien some of yours, Max.'

The three children were each carrying a plastic bag. Max's looked the heaviest. Lucien put out his hands and Max poured pine-cones into them. Most of them fell on the ground, but neither of them bothered. All four children ran off in the direction Sylvie and Lucien had been going in. The two women followed them.

'You were on your way back home,' said Sylvie.

'It doesn't matter,' said Maude. 'As long as we're not complaining or fighting, I don't care. I can't get

210

anything done while they're under my feet. How was Christmas?'

She had got in first with that too.

'Busy,' said Sylvie. 'It all seemed to go all right.'

Lucien and Max were weaving in and out of the trees calling out to each other. The little girls were running after them.

'We had my brother over. It was our turn. Two of his kids went down with flu. Only mild. They carried on eating.'

'Room service,' said Sylvie. 'That must have been tiring.'

'My brother's very good. He kept whipping up and down stairs. I just hope none of the grandparents caught it.'

'They've gone now, have they?'

'Alain's parents have. Mine are staying over New Year to baby-sit for us.'

'Are you doing something nice?'

'A colleague of Alain's is giving a party. It'll make a change.'

Sylvie admired the way she went boldly to the edge. Maude had done New Year's Eve with them last year. It had been livelier than usual. Gingered up by adultery, as she'd realised afterwards. The sort of people who came to the Meuse for the occasion believed that, barring accidents, one year was much like another. Sylvie could see it in their faces when the clock struck. They raised their glasses and some exchanged kisses. Dinner began at nine. Sylvie concentrated all her efforts on prolonging the day, which would have been easy to do in June, but needed contrivance in mid winter. Clients coming down the stairs at six o'clock, in need of a drink, were surprised to see Natalie going round with the hoover. Sylvie, wearing a cardigan and skirt that couldn't be interpreted as smart for evening, asked them if they were looking for a cup of tea. She changed later. The English sometimes accepted the tea, but the others retreated upstairs to the mini bar and the conservative comfort of the bedrooms. Last year Maude's enthusiasm had made it seem more like a party. Then, on New Year's Day, Sylvie had found out why.

'I've been thinking about you,' Maude said. 'It must have been difficult for you.'

'I suppose so,' said Sylvie.

'Missing your Dad,' said Maude.

So that was what she was talking about, Sylvie thought.

'I never really saw him at Christmas.' It was a frosty response.

'It's not just that, though, is it?' said Maude. 'It's a funny time of year. Everything sort of gets stirred up. The whole family thing. It must have felt awful going back to London on your own to sort things out.'

'I didn't really sort anything.'

'Why should you? You need to take your time. Don't take any notice of what anyone else is telling you. Yvette and people,' said Maude. 'What's the point in rushing things? You only end up doing stuff that doesn't feel right and then having to re-do it.'

Sylvie thought, this woman's got a nerve, but listening to her wasn't as grating as it might have been. Part of her felt like responding guardedly. Maybe not even guardedly. In the circumstances, what could they be talking about?

'I miss getting his letters,' she said. 'Usually I'd

212

be getting one in the next few days telling me about his Christmas. He always dressed it up. Made it sound all right. He has these neighbours, well, friends, I suppose, who ask him in for one of the days. They're kind but dull. And he cooked for himself on the other day. His own mother's sort of food it seemed to be, austerity, make do and mend, not Eve's, certainly not Paul's. But he must have been lonely.'

'I was sorry about his last letter.'

'What about it?'

'Paul told me.'

'What did he tell you?'

'The day after you got back from George's funeral. You asked me what I'd done with the post while you'd been away. I knew you were expecting something in particular. I asked Paul about it. Nosy, I know. I'm sorry.'

'I probably made too much of it. I kept asking people. The postman clearly thought I was loopy.' In attempting lightness, Sylvie's voice sounded tinny inside her head, thin in the outdoor air.

'Why shouldn't you make a fuss about it? He was your Dad. I'd have done the same.'

Sylvie glanced sideways at Maude. She looked entirely sincere. This is her famous empathy, she thought. But she felt how it worked.

'He shouldn't have done it,' said Maude.

'Sorry? What shouldn't he have done?' said Sylvie.

'Got rid of it,' said Maude. 'I told him he shouldn't have. I was quite shocked.'

'Your Dad's letter,' said Maude, as Sylvie said nothing. 'I said he had no right to. It wasn't his, after all.'

Sylvie still said nothing.

'He told you, didn't he? Paul? I told him to tell you. He thought you were upset enough. He hates you to be upset, but I said he should do it. I mean, I know it was too late to do anything about it, but then at least you knew.'

'Yes,' said Sylvie. 'He did tell me.'

She said it, because she didn't want Maude to know that he hadn't done; it was as simple as that. But she went cold inside and her heart knocked higher and higher in her chest until she couldn't swallow.

And the small amount of air that was left, she pushed to her brain, where it could only throw out shallow logic in a random manner. She thought, she's been honest with me and now I haven't been honest with her. And coming close behind, but not quite synchronised, she thought, why should I let her think that Paul does exactly what she tells him? Which brought her to the same point, but contradicted it in spirit. And all the time her mind slithered over the surface of the conversation she was having with Maude. She set aside the letter; the real letter which had existed and which she'd ahnost given up on, and the imagined onc, which might have provided the solution. She set Paul aside too.

'Are you all right?' said Maude.

Sylvie saw her, wrapped in her vivid winter coat, self contained and pampered in front of the practical pines. She sounded concerned but unaffected; she couldn't keep that out of her voice. What they were talking about was on the very edge of Maude's own life. Sylvie thought, she doesn't know what she's saying, she's like a child playing

214

with a knife. But she also thought, her dealings with me in general haven't been honest, why should I tell her the truth? She let it stand.

'Yes,' said Sylvie. 'I don't like thinking about it. Still.'

'I'm not surprised,' said Maude.

And having lied, Sylvie couldn't now ask, as she might have done, whether Paul had read the letter and what it had said.

CHAPTER TWELVE

The architecture was incongruous, with its outcrops of turrets and wrought iron and fancy brickwork. A bright blue sky would have browbeaten it, but against the grey clouds and the out-of-season sea, it looked moderately dashing, and there were plenty of places for seagulls to perch.

'I like it here,' Sylvie said. She had to raise her voice to be heard above the wind. They had parked on a side street that led down to the front. The street was respectable and temperamentally closed in, but it ended in the North Sea. She locked the car and walked round onto the pavement. A brass plaque with a dentist's name and qualifications was embedded in the dark hedge next to her. The gate through to the garden was taller than a person and padlocked. A dog ran out and yapped and snapped at the bars.

'I've been stuck inland all my life apart from holidays and there haven't been many of them. Oh, and trips to London,' she said.

'London,' he said. 'I didn't realise that was on the sea.'

'More so than where we come from. It's tidal.'

'It's all right here, once we get on the front,' he said. 'A bit concrete.'

'I can overlook that. It smells of fish and frying. Nearly English.'

'We could try and find some,' he said. 'Have to be careful not to break a tooth. We wouldn't want to disturb Dr Diploma.'

They walked down the road past other hedges. He walked on the outer side of the pavement, in the old fashioned way, as George used to, and, when they crossed over and turned right, he took up the same position. Outside in the daylight and open air he was different from how she remembered him. He seemed to know where he was going. They passed half a dozen shops shuttered for the winter, then he stopped by a door with a lace curtain hanging on the inside of the glass and opened it for her.

'Let's go in here,' he said. 'Get out of the wind.'

*   *   *

There were a few tables to the side of the bar. Sylvie took off her coat and hung it on the clothes stand near the door. He put his on the back of a chair, waited for her to join him. They both sat down. There was no one else there, just a man drying up behind the bar. It was quiet; nothing but an occasional car passing and the chink of the glass. After a few minutes the man came over to them.

'Lunch?' he said patting out a white paper cloth in front of them and banging down two upside down glasses and two clutches of cutlery. He went away again.

The windows were steamed up.

'Home from home, isn't it?' said Sylvie, looking at her companion across the table. She put both her hands on the ornate radiator beside her. It was giving out heat but the cast iron was thick. Her hands looked thin and pale, almost creamy at the tips.

'I don't do lunches,' he said.

'No, I remember that now,' she said. 'Not even boiled eggs. You've been here before though?'

'I drop by two or three times a year. My sister's down here. I don't want to spend the whole day with her. I just call in and say hullo to her and the kids. We could go round later. See if she's in.'

It would be difficult to make this man non-plussed, but Sylvie wondered whether he wasn't. His name was Jacques and he kept the Bar des Sports in the nearby town. They were more than three hundred kilometres from home.

'So you're in those books are you, saying it's safe to go in and eat?' he said.

'One or two of them.'

'What do they say about you? . . . Nestling between a volcano and a reservoir.'

'Perched on slightly raised ground. Yes, that sort of thing. You've got the idea.'

'I can see you in that "Calm and Silence" book. You seem calm and silent. Maybe not calm. I don't know you well enough to judge. Silent, certainly.'

'I thought I was being quite chatty.'

'No,' he said. 'I found it pretty hard going coming down in the car with you. But don't worry about it.'

'I'm not,' she said and thought, that's put me in my place.

'What are you escaping from, then?'

'I thought I was just having a day out.'

He took a packet of cigarettes out of his shirt pocket, shook it, and offered it to her. She shook her head. He took one out and lit it, turned round and stretched out for the ashtray on the next table.

'Go on. Try,' he said. 'Nothing terrible will happen.'

'I don't want to talk about it,' she said. 'But it's not for the reasons you think.'

'What might they be?'

'Isn't there such a thing as just having a day out?'

'No such thing,' he said. 'You've got to earn it.'

'I wouldn't have associated you with a strong work ethic.'

'Associated.' He seemed to savour it. 'You like words like that, don't you?'

'I can't use words *and* be silent, can I?'

'Make your mind up. Is that what you're trying to say. Well, fair enough. I don't mind if you talk to me like that. No, what I meant was, you've got to earn it *with me.*'

The man at the bar came round their side again and put a basket of bread in between them. He said he could offer them a steak or fish. Sylvie said fish.

'You walk in, unannounced, as you'd say. Make that two please, and we'll have some wine. White, whatever you've got.'

'No,' she interrupted. 'I wouldn't say that.'

'Well, anyway, you walk in and say, you woke up and thought a trip to the Belgian seaside seemed a nice idea.'

'You make me sound about ten years old.'

'Something like that. Appealing with it. Really.'

'I don't have that dreadful voice, though.'

'No? Try listening to yourself. No, I'm being unfair. You weren't that bad. Do you make a habit of this sort of thing?'

'No.'

'But you've done something like this before?'

Sylvie was going to say no, again, but she changed her mind.

'Yes,' she said. 'I have done.'

219

'How often?'

'Once.'

'So what did you do? Did you phone first or just show up, like you did with me?'

Sylvie thought, I wrote a letter, but I can't say that.

'I wrote a letter,' she said.

'You *are* straight out of the past, aren't you? How did it turn out?'

'Fine.'

'Fine,' he imitated her, then carried on in his own voice. 'What was he called? No, on second thoughts I don't want to know. You were lucky, that's all.'

'You mean I might have met a murderer. That's a bit over dramatic isn't it?'

'He might have told you you were a silly bitch.'

'As you're doing.'

'No, I wouldn't do that. He'd be worse than me. I've got your best interests at heart. And I like your face.'

'Thanks.'

'No, I mean it,' he said.

She had been going to say, he didn't insult me. He was another human being, nothing complicated. I didn't think I was in love with him, and I didn't lose my nerve.

'Seriously,' he said, 'You need to be careful. What were you about to say just then? Your expression changed.'

He looked at her, as he had done when she was sitting at a separate table in the Bar des Sports, but here he was closer, noticing, it seemed, every shadow that passed. She thought, I'll get back in one piece from this. There was no reason why she shouldn't.

'You go about with some in-built security system, don't you? It's in your face, you never stop thinking. Yet you do these things. You slip the bolt. Dangerous.'

He carried on, 'I'll tell you a story. The first time I came here, I thought, what a lot of pretty waitresses, they can't all be his daughters.' He had put on a self-mocking voice. 'There were three of them. Slips of things. It was fairly busy. They took the orders. Nothing happened, which was funny, as this is basically a fast food sort of place. Well, you can see that for yourself. It's not fancy. Then the penny dropped that one by one the girls had gone upstairs and not come back down again. I was sitting here, waiting for my dinner, with my feet under the table and the boss creeping about looking after me.'

He hadn't lowered his voice and Sylvie looked at the man behind the bar. He was reading a newspaper leaning on his elbows.

'Don't worry about him,' he said. 'You can get it wrong, is what I'm trying to tell you. You think you live in the real world, and then you find out you're missing a slice, or three.'

'I know exactly what I'm missing,' said Sylvie and, before he had time to pick up on that, she looked away from him and scanned the room. 'I can't see the stairs. Where are they?'

He looked over his shoulder. She looked in the same direction. At the end of the bar there was a half-glazed door. The paint was badly scratched. Almost immediately beyond it, she could see what looked like an outhouse with a tin roof and an empty bird cage hanging from a hook. He turned

221

back.

'They were in that corner. He must have got rid of them in the clean up. Made upstairs self contained.'

'That door looks as if it's always been there.'

'That's to fool you. Roughed up with wire wool and a blunt pair of scissors to make it look as if an Alsatian's been jumping up at it for the last ten years. It's all in the mind. What's past and what isn't.'

The boss came across with a jug of wine. He turned their glasses right side up and filled them. He banged the jug on the table. Then he went away through a gap in the shelves of bottles behind the bar. It was only just man sized, draped on both sides with fat curtains pulled tight at their waists. He reappeared with their food on two plates.

'Here's to better days,' Sylvie's companion said. 'I'm sorry I had a go at you.'

'That's all right,' Sylvie said.

'So, are you going to tell me?'

'No,' said Sylvie. 'I'm not.'

She thought, something happened yesterday which made me feel my life weighed a feather. I wanted to do something that matched that feeling. Even if it only lasted a day.

She said. 'I shouldn't have involved anyone else. I was stupid. I'm sorry.'

'Lucky it was me,' he said. 'I didn't even remember you when you walked in this morning, do you know that?'

She might have said, 'I don't believe you,' but she didn't because the conversation would have ended differently, and the day as well. She didn't know, now, if that had been what she wanted.

Jacques had shut the bar for her. Waited until an old fellow had finished his drink, then locked up and left a note on the door saying, Back later, Works outing. Immediately she had felt lighter, having more leverage. She could picture Jacques now, as he was when she turned up at nine o'clock that morning. He was keeping his eye on the television, placed high on brackets, in a corner of the room. A woman was on her haunches, shouting into the face of a man lying on a beach towel. Jacques had glanced at Sylvie but carried on pouring a bottle of beer for a customer, as much as would fill the glass without it overflowing.

'What was that woman going on about this morning? The one on the beach,' she said.

'Don't ask me. It's been going on for weeks. Twice a week. Every now and then one of them stands up.'

'Talking of the past.'

'Were we?' he said.

'You keep the Bar des Sports looking as it would have done twenty years ago. It has the same atmosphere. I felt it as soon as I walked in.'

'I don't tinker around with it,' he said. 'I dislike it in the same way that I dislike myself. We're all of a piece.'

'That sounds comforting,' she said.

'I can't afford to do it up. That's the other explanation. So how's your place?'

'You mean the look of it?' She knew he didn't want general remarks about refurbishment but she needed to know what he was getting at. She wouldn't launch herself into scene painting or restaurant publicity.

'Well, put it another way. How do you spend

223

your days?'

'Starting from first thing in the morning?'

'I meant the feel of it, really.'

She stared at him.

'Don't look so worried,' he said. 'It's only words.'

She waited, too tense to conjure up a description. Then she said, and she didn't know where the words came from, 'I go from complete inactivity—I don't mean lying around in bed—though I have done that—I mean, living the days as if they were rooms I can't get out of—to making a dash for the door.'

He nodded. 'I thought it was something like that.'

She was surprised. It hadn't seemed clear when she said it. She wondered whether to start to explain that she had had her father's funeral to go to, that it hadn't all been escape.

'Why do you go back?' he said, 'I take it you do go back.'

'Oh, yes. I go back.'

'Well?'

'I don't know.'

'Take your time, next time,' he said. 'Over leaving, I mean, not over going back. Do it slowly.'

She thought, it's all right for him to say that. Slowly comes easily to him.

'How am I supposed to do that?' she said.

'Smile inanely and keep shrugging your shoulders. A woman did it to me once. It was very effective. No. That's not fair. I don't know. It all happens between the door and the street.'

*   *   *

On the way back, Jacques fell asleep in the car. They had gone straight from the café to his sister's. He hadn't liked her idea of walking on the beach in the east wind. His sister had been friendly. She hadn't been curious about Sylvie, just got her children to say hullo, and cleared a space on the sofa for her to sit down among the multi-coloured clutter. The television was on and the children ran in and out with drinks that slopped onto the floor. Jacques and his sister talked and Sylvie listened to them. They had the same intonation, the same fairly rapid drawl. She joined in from time to time. It felt peaceful being there.

At the first set of traffic lights coming back into town Jacques woke up. She dropped him outside the bar. He said he wouldn't ask her in for a drink as they were queuing outside. She said she could see that. The road was deserted.

CHAPTER THIRTEEN

'We saw Maude when we were out for a walk, did Lucien tell you?'

'When was that?' Paul said.

'The day before yesterday.'

Lucien was sitting on a high stool, having an early lunch in the restaurant kitchen. The two boys, who had come in to help for New Year's Eve, were working at the far end of the long counter, heads bent, wrists and forearms moving rapidly. Dried figs were cooking slowly in the oven in some sort of liquor, smelling good with the mustiness of old clothes. The smell didn't match the bright overhead lights or the efficient activity.

'Do you want that cut up?' Paul said.

'No,' said Lucien.

'Aren't you going to say anything?' Sylvie said.

Lucien looked up quickly and saw she was talking to Paul. The oven emitted a low hum but none of the kitchen machines was running. The boys slapped pastry down and it made the right sort of sound, elastic, like flesh.

'How was she?' he said. The boys didn't slow down.

'She was well,' Sylvie said. 'Extremely well. She said her brother had been over for Christmas and that his kids had gone down with flu. It didn't seem to have put them out too much. She said they were bored with their presents and that they had two kittens. I couldn't make out whether the kittens had been presents and they were bored with them too. She said things weren't going too well with

226

them and the dog.'

'They weren't presents,' said Lucien. 'They just got them.'

'They might have come from the farm,' Sylvie said. 'They've always got spare kittens.'

'I hope you're enjoying this, Sylvie,' Paul said. His voice wasn't loud but the boys, stamping out pastry, might have been able to hear what he said.

'I am,' said Sylvie.

'You've made your point. You can stop now,' he said.

'But I haven't told you what Maude said yet.'

'I think that had better wait.' He glanced at Lucien. 'You've put yourself back in the right.'

*   *   *

She hadn't given any explanation about her day away with Jacques. She had parked the car and gone straight to her bedroom to change her clothes. Then she had gone to the kitchen to tell Paul she was home and that she would be on duty for the end of dinner. He had asked her where she'd been and she'd said, 'Out,' and gone into the dining room. Felix was skating between tables with coffee and bills and the last of the puddings. He had ignored her.

She had been tired driving home and had kept making small errors. She had been lucky that nothing worse had happened than being mouthed at by moon-faced drivers. Jacques had slept through it. Once she was back in the restaurant she kept thinking of George. She saw him go to the cupboard for a block of writing paper and sit down at the table to write to her, then get up, put on his coat, go out, lock the front door, walk to the post box, post the letter. This was the last action in the sequence, then she went back to the beginning, the cupboard, the writing paper, the table, the coat; so it continued.

She said, 'Maude was telling me what had happened to George's letter.'

'Which letter?' Paul said. He had gone back to his preparations and was turned away from her. Brushing quails with clarified butter.

'The one I asked the postman about.'

'Why was she talking about that?'

'We hadn't got anything better to talk about.'

'It was none of her business.'

'I'm glad she did. It was neighbourly of her.'

'You're not still bothered about it, are you?'

Sylvie thought, the letter has gone. When Maude said he had thrown it away, it broke free, but not George with it. He had spent the best part of one of the last hours in his life, writing it, maybe longer. He had expected her to get it. He had gone to the trouble of posting it. It had probably been raining. He would have taken his umbrella. She hadn't included that in her sequence.

She said, 'I still think about it, yes.'

'I thought we'd been through all this. I thought we were making some kind of progress. This is really depressing.'

He paused for a moment and poured hot water into a bowl of dried mushrooms, then he picked up the brush again.

'It's a nuisance to you, isn't it? Death and everything about it.'

Paul didn't acknowledge that she had spoken. He walked away to the other side of the room. He stood over the boys, who were chopping leeks, separating the white from the green, and waited while they finished their task, then he gesticulated at the heavy-duty food processor and the clock on the wall with its large roman numerals. One of the boys switched it on. The machine stared to whirr. The noise was loud and serviceable. Paul walked back across the kitchen and stood right beside her.

'Sylvie, I have no idea what you mean by that; these are just words you're using to be offensive. It is New Year's Eve. I cannot waste time.'

'It would be nice to have the letter back, that's all. It makes for completeness. I've got all his others. He "bothered", as you say to write to me. He expected me to get it. One day I'll sit down and read all his letters through. I read all mine to him when I was in London. Did I tell you? They didn't make good reading. I'd no idea I was as small-minded as that. Small-minded and somehow pathetic. They jollied along like some updated nursery rhyme. You know those awful songs Lucien used to learn in nursery school. Not off the wall, like the traditional English ones, just banal and tiresome.'

'Why did you say something about me? What songs are you talking about?' Lucien said.

'I'll see if I can remember one later; they weren't very memorable,' Sylvie said.

'I didn't sing them. I don't like singing.'

'Sylvie.'

'Yes, Paul?'

'You must let it go. It doesn't exist. This isn't doing you any good.'

'No?'

'No.'

unoccupied theatre or a concert hall because it reverted to something more like home; more dismal because of that. Clean sepulchral cloths, high-backed chairs squared up at the tables, Christmas greenery still hanging on with its evergreen staying power. Red anemones in the table vases for New Year's Eve. Otherwise bare; no glasses, no cutlery, no artificial light, no bottles, no food. It was what Sylvie saw every day between meals. She knew the rhythm of it. In a few hours' time it would come alive. But that made no difference to the desolation of how it was now. She looked round. For a moment, the way it used to look came back to her. The room under the old dispensation of the brother and sister. The odd pieces of carpet and home-made rugs, the runner, edged with tatting, tacked to the mantelpiece, the old hand sewing machine, pairs of binoculars, appliquéd pictures, things that harboured dust, hiding places.

'Excuse me.'

They both turned. A woman was poised between the hall and the dining room. Her feet were holding back on the threshold but her head and upper body were leaning forward.

Paul let go of Sylvie's hand and walked towards the woman. She remained fixed in the doorway, wearing a short outdoor coat and holding a bag behind her legs. She waited until he was close.

'My mother has special dietary requirements. She's brought her own food and we're wondering if we could put it in a fridge. I've been waiting in the lobby to ask someone but there doesn't seem to be anyone about.'

'I shall be happy to make something special for

your mother, if you tell me what she can and can't eat,' Paul said, 'but I'm afraid she won't be able to eat her own food in my restaurant.'

'It won't be any trouble,' the woman said. 'It's been prepared.'

'It would be for us,' Sylvie said.

'I said they might not like me going in their kitchen.'

'You were quite right,' Sylvie said.

'What am I supposed to do with it? It's all in the cool bag.'

'If you give it to me,' Sylvie said, putting her hand out, 'I'll see to it for you.'

'What do you mean, see to it?'

'Get rid of it,' Sylvie said. She saw the woman's expression. 'The food, I mean, I'll give the bag straight back to you.'

'No,' the woman said.

'Well, if you'd prefer, I'll keep it for you until you leave. How long are you staying?'

'We booked, I can assure you.'

'Of course,' Sylvie said.

'My mother's still in the car. At least she didn't go to the trouble of getting out. We won't be able to stay now.'

She didn't move. She stared at the bare tables.

'We're sorry,' Sylvie said, 'but, of course, it's your choice.'

The woman seemed to her to be rootless and homeless in spite of her demands. Arriving from nowhere and with nowhere to go. The loneliness of this moment could go on for ever. Sylvie had to make herself think of a house full of furniture, televisions, pot plants, cats; anything to provide this stranger with the usual comforts.

233

'I shall be contacting the brochure,' the woman said. 'You couldn't tell me which number room we would have had, could you?'

'Certainly,' Sylvie said. 'Seven.'

'Seven,' the woman said. 'I collect numbers.'

'It's lucky,' Sylvie said.

The woman took one last look round and walked back through the hall and out of the main door. They heard her footsteps going across the gravel.

'Thank you, Sylvie. You saved me a lot of hassle,' Paul said. 'New Year's Eve too. What a joke.'

'It wasn't me,' Sylvie said. 'It was one of those situations that sorts itself out.'

'Was it seven?'

'I've no idea.'

Paul smiled. They heard the car engine start and the car moving away.

'Do you want me to do anything for you?' he said.

'I don't think so.'

'I'll go and get on, then.'

'Tell Lucien I'll be along in a minute.'

Sylvie saw that Paul was relieved that the woman had intervened and that she had been capable of talking rationally to her. Not rationally, effectively. It was the way she talked to the clients. He appreciated what she did, while thinking it could have been less peculiar. She brought out the strangeness in them. But they had never had any trouble with clients in all the years they'd been here.

There was nothing Sylvie wanted from him. She could make him put his hand in the bottom of the clock case or behind the mirror over the mantelpiece. She could make him feel the emptiness. What the living shared with the dead was nothing; not absolute nothing, which she couldn't comprehend, but the emptiness through which life flowed.

People talked of extracting apologies as though they were teeth and what they were left with was a mouth full of blood and a sore jaw. So she would forget it, as Paul had asked her to, but it wouldn't mean the same thing as he meant by it. Whatever guilt had been visible in his face had been cleaned off since Maude had slipped out of the conversation.

The woman and her mother would be back on the main road. Everywhere would be booked up for tonight. Sylvie imagined them driving home without discussion, retracing their steps, thinking that the route looked nearly identical the other way on, like a sock turned inside out.

She went to the bookshelf in the hall where they kept guide books for the use of the guests. She changed them every year. In their business there was nothing worse than old dates on display. She took one out and ran her finger down a page and, holding the book open, dialled a telephone number. Then, after she'd finished the call and put the receiver down she went to see if Lucien had finished his lunch.

CHAPTER FOURTEEN

Sylvie didn't get further than Calais on the evening of January 1. The hotel she checked into was tall and thin, with metal windows and a lift like the inside of a cheese grater. Lucien was interested in it and in the signed notice of its annual check. He wasn't any trouble. He had sat, with his seat belt on, in the back of her car, asking her questions about the flares from the oil refinery and the bikers lined up in the service station. He hadn't been on many long journeys. They had gone to a café, in the centre of town, for a late-night snack and had chosen a table by the window. Across the road was a doorway framed in multi-coloured lights. It must have been the entrance to a bar or a club, but it didn't have a name. Lucien wanted to know who would come out of it. Sylvie said he would have to keep looking. Eventually a man came out. He turned into the alley between that building and the next and punched someone who was crouching on the bottom step of some stone stairs. Then he went back through the doorway again. 'They'll put those Christmas lights away in a box soon; they'll do it when we take the Christmas tree down,' Lucien told her. She said she thought they wouldn't. They looked permanent. Then, a minute later, he said, 'The police will come and get that man. Why didn't he run away?' but she had no explanation. Two men came out of another door and bent over the victim. The ambulance turned up about ten minutes later and the crew bundled him in and drove off.

The room was adequate and the bed shallow. Lucien's head on the pillow was a beautiful curve; his neck, little but sturdy. Sylvie left the main light on. There wasn't a bedside lamp. He wouldn't wake up. He was deeply asleep. She had already drawn the curtains and shut out the street. The fabric was familiar; a safe hotel pattern that was dated before it went up but would last fifteen years. She would always notice that sort of thing. It was part of what she knew. She cleaned off her make-up, brushed her teeth and had a shower. Nothing took long. She allowed the bathroom and the bedroom to merge, wandered between them. She needed to walk, though the distance was short, just up and down. She saw her face in two mirrors; the one in the bathroom more exacting, but the looks shared between them. Tired French, tired English, troubled, untroubled, astonished at what she was doing.

Sylvie lay down next to Lucien, found the light switch and put it off. She had done New Year's Eve. Hospitality and impeccable service. Every guest got to bed, or out to a car. Every table stripped down and relaid. The dining room aired. The night had been short, but she had managed to sleep. She had been surprised to find that she had. First a dream, and then the morning.

There was noise outside here. Bursts of shouting. Irregular footsteps. Car tyres. It was all subdued and over quickly. Tonight's boozing just a top up. Someone further down the street must have had a window open, letting in the weather, because she could hear a female vocalist, perfect, relayed electronically, then, afterwards, a real woman singing. Internal doors in the hotel banged shut;

thin doors with noisy fastenings. Water knocked in the pipes. In the next room, a man and a woman carried on talking.

She hadn't given Paul reason to panic. She had told him that she was taking Lucien to London before school started again. School was a reassuring word as long as you weren't in it. He would hang on to the safety of it. She would call him when she got to George's flat. She had told him after breakfast. She said she'd be leaving in an hour, or so, and would take her time to get there. They would stay a night by the sea, one side or the other. That sounded more contingent than saying Calais or Dover. They would go on the boat. She had had enough of the Tunnel and Lucien would prefer it. Paul thought it was about Maude, some delayed resentment. She'd allowed him to think it. He had kissed them both goodbye and waved as they drove away. No one else knew. He would have to tell Yvette. Without Maude, or Sylvie, he'd need her to help him. Sylvie didn't know what he would say. Yvette would ask a lot of questions and, as the days went by, would ask more, developing a sense of unease and intense curiosity, simultaneously. She would strain her imagination to get it right, seeing Sylvie in a distant room, probably uncomfortable, as it was George's, hardly space to turn round. A good daughter, all those letters she used to write to him, but not doing her best by Lucien, taking him away from his home, like that, to an old man's flat without any toys. Not doing her best by her own son either. Putting the dead before the living. Yvette would have imagined her lying beside Paul for ever. For a short time she would find it painful to think of Sylvie outside the familiar

238

limits. Then the words would return. Sylvie was acting out of character, she'd come back home. Or, there was always something odd about Sylvie, that didn't quite fit; she wasn't surprised at this turn of events. They were two sides of the same thought. It was harder to conceive of the narrow space that was truly someone else and unpredictable to other people. Because, to get at it, whoever was doing the thinking, had to concentrate in a way that went through and beyond what looked fixed, through and beyond the faces and gestures, ways of walking and talking, and the forms that were known off by heart.

*   *   *

Sylvie closed her eyes. It was already the second day of January. Dark for the moment but light again in a few hours. She didn't have a ticket or know the times of the crossings. They would follow the signs to the docks and join a queue. The morning would be damp and dull. It wouldn't feel like the beginning of a holiday, or a year; not the beginning of anything.

*   *   *

George wouldn't have gone to Don's for New Year. Don was kind enough, and Judith. George appreciated what they did for him, but he wouldn't have wanted to be there. He would have walked to the row of shops nearby, past the wine bar and the dry cleaners. Both shut. He would have bought some milk and a loaf for toast from the perpetual grocer; eight until ten. Long hours. But the man never exerted himself. No one had ever seen him away from the chair. George would have taken a different route back, adding in side streets to get a bit of exercise. He would have had a book waiting for him at home and a bottle, a couple of pounds dearer than usual, to mark the change in the date. Eve would have been there in spirit, lovely to look at and almost too much for him.

Everything on the cross Channel ferry would be lightweight, capable of floating—paper cups, plastic spoons, newsprint, empty packaging—the boat itself smelling of sea water and cheap coffee, just solid enough to contain them. Sylvie would be with Lucien, who was a child, and strangers who wouldn't know that this was the state of things.

When they reached the other side, they would drive through Kent, then through the London suburbs from east to west. She knew the route, and although, in one way, she was glad of this, in another, she was sorry that she wouldn't have to worry about finding the way.